Nobbut

Nobbut

Nancy Moody

The Pentland Press Limited
Edinburgh • Cambridge • Durham • USA

First published in 1996 by
The Pentland Press Ltd.
1 Hutton Close
South Church
Bishop Auckland
Durham

British Library Cataloguing in Publication Data.
A Catalogue record for this book is available
from the British Library.

ISBN 1 85821 419 x

Typeset by CBS, Felixstowe, Suffolk
Printed and bound by Antony Rowe Ltd., Chippenham

CONTENTS

FOREWORD

I am pleased to write the foreword to this fascinating book which is a glimpse into the life of its author, a lady whom I have known as a friend and neighbour for 45 years. As the story unfolds the reader will find a person of great integrity accompanied by a charming outgoing personality.

Nancy's early years, spent in rural Nottinghamshire in a caring and loving home, albeit one which suffered hardship and privation, were followed by two years of teacher training in London. These years prepared her for the difficulties and tragedies of the Second World War which she faced with courage and resolution. During this time and afterwards she helped her husband to establish himself in his profession.

The years which followed were fulfilled by a happy marriage and the arrival of much loved children. Her love of flowers and gardens and all things beautiful provided relaxation. Nancy developed her talents in music, art and literature and through composing, conducting and performing she contributed to the education and pleasure of young and old.

From time to time Nancy has suffered serious illness, an anxiety for friends and family. Nevertheless her resolution has never weakened when working for something she believes in.

As the reader will readily perceive, Nancy is sustained by a steadfast faith and an interest in care for her fellow men.

This book will not only fascinate but will also be an inspiration to many who can identify with the incidents which Nancy relates.

Isobel Connell.

The pleasures of home, of the countryside, of social intercourse, of quick feelings, and of serious and many-sided activity, fill up the overflowing measure of joyous and useful life. The daily round and common task, are irradiated with a glory from beyond land or sea, and are transformed into the palace of a king.

CHAPTER ONE

END AND BEGINNING

'Half a stone, love, when you've minute,' Fred beamed across the counter at Annie. 'No need to hurry, I've plenty of time and I'm enjoying the view.'

Annie gave him a look which would have quelled most of her male acquaintances, but which seemed to have the reverse effect upon Fred Finch. 'Half-day, ain't it?' he added with a wink. 'Going to watch the cricket on the Plain Piece? I'm having a stroll up there myself if you're short of an escort.'

Annie was furious, but she managed a reasonably polite, 'I'm not very interested in cricket, thank you, Fred,' and weighed his sugar as hastily as possible.

'You might grow to like it, and me, if you gave yourself a chance. There's sometimes better fish in t'local stream than in t'bigger rivers, tha knaws.'

That was the worst of Fred. You couldn't shake him off, and when his speech slipped into the vernacular he was obviously sincere in what he said.

He must have heard through that old gossip Liza Hawkins that Weldon had not been over for two weeks.

Fred paid the coppers for his armful of sugar and went back to his bakery. He threw Annie a look of mingled pity and genuine affection. His case was hopeless and he knew it, but he couldn't help teasing her and enjoying the flash in her eyes and the little toss of annoyance of her gypsy-black curls. He'd see her tomorrow when he delivered the bread for the party at the Town Hall.

'After all,' he considered, 'I'm not a bad catch. I'm my own boss and the best baker in the town. I'll mebbe die youngish, as my dad did. Baking's

1

not a healthy life, but wi' Annie to sing wi' and to give me a few bairns it would be a merry life, if a short one.'

When he was out of sight Annie's father emerged from the tiny office in the corner of the shop. He'd heard all that had been said and knew what turbulent emotions had been stirred in Annie's breast.

'Fred's not a bad lad. Bit rough, but he means well. Good tenor voice and a good business. Might do worse. Don't wait love. If there's anything you should be doing at the back I'll manage now.'

Annie adored her father, but she brushed back her tears and fled from the shop up the stairs to her bedroom. Now that Kathie was married and Fran a probationer at the new Cottage Hospital, at least she had a room to herself. It meant a great deal to be alone at times and she threw herself onto the big bed and beat her fists angrily into the pillows.

So even her father would be glad to see her go down the street and live in the sickly-smelling bakery! The rooms above were well-furnished and carpeted and Fred was generous and would be kind in his way, but the thought of spending years in this street she'd grown to hate, with Fred's cough getting worse and the nauseating smell of the bakery permeating every corner was more than she could contemplate. Besides, he was going bald already and the thought of his puffy hands touching her was abhorrent.

No, she would rather be an old maid if Weldon let her down.

She got up from the bed and went to the window. She stared down the long yard with the storehouse at the side, the pump and tiny garden in the middle and the loathsome privy at the far end next to the wall.

She'd grown to hate it all. With Kathie and Fran gone the house was lifeless. Joe helped with the business but had taken to frequenting the Crazy Cow in the evenings. She knew he was seeing a great deal of Maggie Jones and Co. They were a noisy, boozy crowd, but Joe was obviously entangled very deeply with Maggie and would hear no word against them.

'Annie! Nance! Are you up there?' called her mother from the foot of the stairs. 'What are you doing up there in the middle of the morning? I've been at it since six o'clock, and you're up there preening yourself already for your worthless Weldon. He didn't come last week and he'll not come today. Take my word for it, he's too good-looking with his black curls and flashing eyes. He'll have half-a-dozen city lasses throwing themselves at him and be going from one to another like a cock in a farmyard. Have you cleaned the privy? Come on down here and get on with your work.'

Annie bit her lips and ran down the stairs. 'I needed a clean hankie,' she said, as she blew her nose ostentatiously and hoped that her blotchy face would escape her mother's sharp eyes. 'Weldon has a lot of studying to do,' she added. 'He's not going to be a grocer or a baker.'

It was a stupid thing to say and she regretted it as soon as it was out. Her tiny mother's temper was never at its best the day before a big 'do' at the Town Hall. Catering for a hundred or more and providing home-made cakes and pastries, home-cooked hams, tongues and chickens called for endless hours of sheer hard grind coupled with skill and forethought. In sultry July weather meat could go off and cream turn at the eleventh hour. Everything had to be taken by wagonette to the Town Hall and carried up forty stone steps to the banqueting hall. Reliable help had to be hired now that two of her daughters were gone. That stupid Liza Hawkins's rum had been tossed by day-dreaming Annie into the coffee when she grabbed the jug by mistake to use as a ladle last time. The fact that the members of the temperance society who were feasting had approved heartily of the very special coffee had not really compensated for the knowledge that such a thing could happen at one of their banquets. Old Liza had broken two beautiful hand-painted French dessert plates to show how she felt about the loss of her tot, and Annie had had her ears roundly boxed by her mother for not taking more care.

Neither of them looked forward to tomorrow night, although both knew that compliments would be flying thick and fast before the evening was over.

Annie's mother remembered the relief afforded to her feelings by the boxing of Annie's ears and whipped round hastily to repeat the gesture on hearing the implied criticism of the family's status.

Annie dodged on one side and her mother's hand went with full force on the wall. It jarred badly and she was sorry in her turn for flying off so easily at her remaining daughter. The girl was genuinely fond of the handsome young probationer minister and her mother fully understood the sensitive Annie's deep desire to have a home away from the endless demands of a catering business coupled with a grocery store. Her own passion was singing, and her weekly lesson with the organist and choir-master was Annie's greatest pleasure.

Both parents were singers. The huge, deep-chested black-bearded Tom had a rich bass voice which matched his impressive presence. Ann's voice was light and flexible and much appreciated in the church choir.

Annie's lessons were considered a luxury and she paid for them herself. Half of her weekly allowance of three shillings went in this way. Another sixpence for the church collection and little was left for personal extravagances such as peppermints or the more exotic floral gums.

Annie was often asked to sing at concerts and her beautiful soprano would touch the hearts of old and young alike. When she shared the platform with more experienced professional singers she was conscious of their jealous looks when the prolonged clapping called her back for second encores. But Tom would not consider letting her train as a professional. 'Your voice is a gift from God and you must give the pleasure of it to others,' he insisted, so the modest fees offered to her had to be refused.

There were times when her love of her father paled into insignificance beside her burning desire to develop her talent and travel abroad singing to the world.

Annie ran to the scullery to grab the pail and brush she needed for her most loathed chore. Before she was free to please herself when the shop closed for half a day she had to face the task of scrubbing out the wooden-topped privy. She poured hot water from the huge iron kettle into the pail, cooled it with some from the pump in the yard and dragged herself wearily up the path. There were rambler roses and honeysuckle growing round the door of the privy and she stopped to smell them before flinging open the door and beginning her scrubbing.

Once away from the house and shop her spirits rose and she looked forward to the freedom of the afternoon.

Perhaps Weldon and Edwin would come over from Sheffield after all. It was a lovely day. She forgot her miserable mood of the morning and began to sing as she went to the wall at the end of the garden and flung the dirty

Grandmother with six children 1882. Annie (Mother), second from left.

water over into the stream on the other side.

'Pity the poor fish!' said a voice from the far end of the yard.

Annie turned and her cheeks flamed as Edwin came towards her. She was wearing the old black apron her father used for plucking hens. Her face was perspiring from her exertions and her mop of hair was over her eyes. 'What? Where? You're very early,' she said, wishing the earth would swallow her up.

Weldon hadn't come, and she knew he would not come again.

Edwin's grey eyes took in all her turbulent emotions. He thought he'd never seen her look more beautiful though he'd loved her from the minute he'd first seen her two years before.

'Where's Weldon?' she asked. 'Have you come alone?'

'I'm really here on business,' he replied. 'I'm thinking of buying a tailoring and outfitting business in the town. I love this little place. It's heaven to come out here after working in Sheffield.'

'Where's Weldon?' Annie repeated, showing no interest in the angular Edwin's plans.

'He can't come. He's very busy . . . Look, lass, you know as well as I do he's let you down.'

Annie's face blanched. 'You mean it's all over between us? Really? Finished for good?'

'Yes, lass. He's got engaged to Mary Blanchford. They've been on and off for years, and this time she's got a ring and told him he's to stop coming over here. I'm sorry, Annie. You didn't deserve it, but I've seen it coming and been tearing my heart out for you.'

She looked at his kind face and believed him. 'Oh well!' she said, and could think of nothing else to say. She picked up her pail and he took it from her.

'Look, Annie, I've hired a wagonette for the day. Come and see my little business. There's a nice house over it and a garden behind. I'll take you for a drive out to Sunnyside and Carlton Lake, and we'll go over to Blyth and have tea.'

The strong sensitive fingers of his free hand took her damp hand in a reassuring grasp. 'I can't say much. Weldon's my friend. I'd never have met your lovely family but for Weldon, but let's both forget him for today. Get your meal quickly. I'll have mine in town and meet you at the Priory Gatehouse at 2 o'clock. Will you come?' He looked at her beseechingly and she saw the love he'd been trying to hide from her.

The sun burnished his dark auburn hair and for once his face was almost handsome.

He wasn't Weldon. She'd never feel completely lost in love for anyone else, she was sure, but her heart went to meet Edwin's kindness and compassion. She nodded her head and went back into the gloomy scullery.

The old clock in the big living kitchen struck once, and the sound was followed immediately by the clatter of the shop blinds dropping down and the grind of the huge key in the door of the Meredith establishment. Big Tom's voice boomed, 'Rocked in the cradle of the deep,' as he strolled into the kitchen and whipped up his tiny wife in his arms. He rocked her like a baby and roared with laughing as she kicked her legs furiously and cried out, 'Put me down, you big black bear. Where's your masonic decorum? You're as bad as you were thirty years ago. I should have married Charlie Aspland.'

'Aye, and been scrimping and saving to make ends meet and suffering fools gladly in case of offending his congregation. I can see you lady of the manse with never a hair out of place!' He tickled her face mercilessly with his huge beard and then put her down very carefully in front of the enormous kitchen range. 'You were meant to conjure marvellous meals for my big brood, little witch. What have you got there, the smell of which has been tantalizing my nostrils for over an hour?'

He kissed the top of her head and then leaned over her, completely blinding her with his beard. Ann whipped round and tickled his ribs till he howled for mercy, and Annie walked quietly in to watch the fun.

'I'm going out with Edwin,' she said, when her voice could be heard. 'I might as well. He's very kind.'

CHAPTER TWO

FAMILY

When it was established that Weldon's affections were engaged elsewhere, Annie gradually accepted the fact and took Edwin's attentions more seriously.

It was not an exciting relationship as far as Annie was concerned, but Edwin was full of fun and very considerate, and she knew in the heart that he was a much finer character than his friend. When he moved into the town and established himself as a first-class tailor and outfitter, his visits to the Meredith household became more frequent, and his courting of Nancy an established fact. He declared he had enough love for the two of them, and she finally agreed to marry him.

By this time Tom Meredith's health had declined and he was desperately ill with gangrene. The wedding date was fixed twice and then cancelled, but he begged them to go ahead the third time. He was only just alive when they returned from the ceremony one raw winter's day, and he died shortly afterwards.

Edwin and his Nancy set up house together over his new business premises in Bridge Place, and she soon came to adore him as much as he did her.

However, Nancy was not a born housekeeper and Edwin's mother's visits were a source of great anxiety to her. The older woman's standards were extremely high, and the atmosphere was tense, when she tackled a job and did it efficiently in half the time it took her dreamy daughter-in-law. Her visits were always followed by very generous gifts as if to compensate for the crisp remarks dropped when she was visiting. Edwin's two sisters, Althea and Ada, were all kindness and generosity, knowing themselves that their mother's over-critical behaviour was a burden to live with.

Mother, aged 15, 1890 – dressed up to sing as a gypsy.

Just within a year of their marriage Tom was born. He was a beautiful child with a mop of fair curls and a very lovable disposition, but alas, he had a defective heart, and needed careful handling. Two years later Alfred Edwin was born. Nancy's health was going down hill and breastfeeding was out of the question, but he thrived on the bottle and was a very contented baby.

Edwin decided that Nancy and Tom would benefit from a move into the country and so they went to live at Sunnyside, a steep climb out of the low-lying town, where the air was much fresher.

Unfortunately Tom's heart made it necessary for him to be carried to the top of the very steep hill where they lived. Douglas made his appearance when Tom was four and nearly drove his good-natured father to drink.

He was lusty, particularly of lung, and more particularly in the middle of the night. As they now lived two miles from the shops Edwin did most of Nancy's shopping and 'never forgot a ribbon nor a button'. He cycled up the long climb to the bottom of Sunnyside and then pushed his cycle up the steep unmade road to their house at the top. Once there, his many duties included caring for the garden, and when Nancy was prostrate with sickness or pregnancy he aspired to such heights as trying to beat a Yorkshire pudding and cook the Sunday joint. Nights spent in 'walking the boards' with his tough little third-born took their toll and he began to age, along with his beloved.

Eric Meredith followed Douglas, and Nancy and Edwin began to despair of having a daughter. Eric was a sunny-natured, 'easy' child and a happy contrast to Douglas. The latter's belligerent nature was often left behind when he went visiting, and he came back from the cranky old maid next door with a penny or an orange whenever he called. She referred to him as 'dear little Duddalons – such a sweet little boy!'

However, after the birth of yet another boy, who lived only two days, Nancy fell pregnant for the sixth time. Her health had declined markedly, and she was dreading the extra burden on her waning strength, but her joy knew no bounds when little Mary was born.

A beautiful contented baby and a girl at last – Edwin's heart burst with joy and gratitude, and for the first time two years passed without another

1895 – Fran with Mother, aged 20, seated.

pregnancy. Mary was an intelligent and adorable child and the light and life of the full household. Nancy's health began to improve and she dared to hope that her family was complete. There had been all the usual children's ailments, but apart from the almost immediate death of the very premature baby boy and the constant anxiety over Tom's weak heart, they had not been unduly unfortunate by the standards of the time.

But in 1913 Eric went down with a sharp attack of scarlet fever and little Mary followed suit. She was not so severely ill but with the other boys to consider the doctor insisted that she must follow Eric to the Isolation Hospital two miles away.

Edwin and Nancy were desolate. The child's attachment to them both was extremely strong, and leaving her in the hands of strangers was an agony. She had been there only a short time when Nancy woke in the early hours of the morning and cried out to Edwin, 'She's gone.'

Alas, it was so! Before breakfast there was a messenger from the hospital to say that she had died – indeed at the time when Nancy had called out to Edwin. The matron at the hospital told them that she had died of grief, not of scarlet fever, and that Eric, who had been extremely ill, had fought desperately for his life and surprised them all by pulling through.

Edwin remained silent and dry-eyed for many weeks, and Nancy knew that his grief was inexpressible. She was relieved when at last in the night she was woken by his sobbing.

She was ill again, and pregnant, when war broke out the following year. There couldn't be another Mary, and she wouldn't dare to love her as much if another girl were born. It was another boy, Denys Lloyd, a sunny – topped little dreamer, loving and lovable and someone to sing to by the fireside.

Having struck once, disaster came again. Edwin's business became difficult because of the war, and then the shop next door was burnt down. What was not damaged by water and fire in Edwin's shop was stolen by people who came to 'help' and his shelves were stripped. There was no hope of replacing things at that time and he was not adequately covered by insurance. He had many friends in the town, indeed his workshop was in the nature of an all-party, ecumenical club, where anyone dropped in for a chat or to discuss problems. His disaster was a source of great sorrow to

Father, 1893, aged 20.

them all.

Most active men in the town had been called up, but Edwin told Nancy they'd winked a blind eye at him 'for family reasons'. She learned the truth later. At any rate, a company firm was glad to have him as manager and to know that his many customers would follow him and patronize their establishments.

The war dragged on, and Edwin bought a plot of land to grow fruit and vegetables and rented two more to keep hens. Pigs and a nanny goat were added to the menage to provide meat and milk, and Edwin's burdens increased with the additional cares. But animals loved him as people did, and it was a happy home. Fun and good humour were the sauce and seasoning of meals when black bread stuck in the throat and Nancy was reduced to performing miracles with plenty of vegetables 'and an old boot!'

But yet another pregnancy in 1916 produced tears of despair and unending weariness. The couple had moved to another house on the main road, with a bigger garden, but it was obvious that there was not room there for an indefinite number of children. Edwin's income was severely reduced since the loss of his own business, and prices were rising. His energy at forty-two was considerably lessened by the strains on all sides. When a second daughter was born at the end of the year their rejoicing was tempered by the fact that she cried for milk that Nancy couldn't supply, and seemed to reflect the growing despair of her mother. She was christened simply Nancy, by which name her mother had always been called by Edwin and her closest friends.

As she pulled round after the pregnancy Nancy regained her interest in life, and with Edwin was in great demand as an entertainer. When she sang to the troops stationed on the Plain Piece her effect on them seemed little short of miraculous, and her moving voice brought thunders of applause. She was very happy then. Edwin had an amazingly good memory and was a very popular actor and elocutionist. After their concerts they returned full of thankfulness to their brood and found some blessings to count.

Neighbours by this time were in the main without the father at home, or they were mourning the loss of sons. Grim-faced, lean men returned for leaves and Nancy felt that she was extremely lucky to have Edwin with

Father (Edwin) with Denys, 1916.

her. She knew that he loved people so much that to have been obliged to go and kill would have destroyed his personality. In spite of all his cares he had always time to put down his own barrow and push someone else's. The war caused him a great deal of mental anguish, but he was spared active participation.

The reason for this was made apparent to Nancy only after the terrible war was over – in fact five days after the Armistice was signed.

Unknown to anyone but Edwin and her closest friends Nancy was pregnant again. She was extremely thin and going down with the dreadful 1918 'flu when invited to a close friend's son's 21st birthday party. He was home on leave and there were great celebrations. Nancy was asked to sing and Edwin to recite, and they had a very happy evening. Within forty-eight hours Nancy was in bed with a very bad attack of the 'flu, and the older boys went down with it at the same time.

Another tiny baby girl was born very prematurely. She weighed three and a half pounds, and the doctor said, 'Don't bother with the baby. She won't live. Look after the mother. She's all the rest of the brood to see to.' But the instincts of a midwife are strong, and the frail little girl was cared for as well as possible in the 'flu stricken household. The nurse booked to attend the confinement was ill, the neighbours were ill, Edwin took the 'flu but had to keep going.

He was found dead in bed when the latest baby was five days old. The doctor told Annie that Edwin had a defective heart and that was why he had not been passed by the board for active service.

Grief, weakness and despair reduced Nancy to a shadow. It had been said of Tom that he would not live to see the age of seventeen. In actual fact he was almost seventeen when he was suddenly obliged to become the man of the family. Edwin's firm gave him a job, but he could not take on the responsibilities carried by his father, and the family income was reduced still further.

By Christmas 1918 Nancy's situation seemed desperate. Joe, her youngest brother invited her to take the family there for the day, and she put the two baby girls in the pram and dragged wearily with her sons round her down into the town and along to her childhood home. The family business had gone downhill rapidly since the death of her father, but there was still comparative plenty and luxury there. Nancy felt that every eye was on her, and that she was an object of pity to the whole town. She recalled her wretchedness at that time to the end of her days.

Douglas was away in Sheffield at the time of his father's death. He had osteo myelitis and was under treatment in the infirmary for a considerable time. He came home with crutches to find that little Nancy was talking and to meet tiny Althea Edwina. His return filled his mother with very mixed feelings. He was rarely out of trouble, and it was soon a joke in the neighbourhood that he could flee from the police or gamekeepers as fast on his crutches as his cronies on two sound feet. He knew the countryside in intimate detail – where every bird nested, where the biggest mushrooms grew and baskets could be filled with blackberries in the shortest time. Other people's apples were always more tempting than those grown by his father and Edwin had felt powerless in his efforts to arouse a conscience in the boy. From an early age he had played truant from school. Edwin had been greeted effusively by his teacher on one occasion, 'Oh, Mr Ilett, thank you so much for the beautiful flowers you sent last week. It is such a pity that Douglas is so prone to sickness.'

'But he's as tough as leather,' said Edwin, 'and I'm afraid you've made a mistake, I didn't send any flowers.'

'But he always brings a beautiful bunch of flowers when he's been sick again,' insisted the young teacher.

'They're not from my garden, and he's never sick,' was the reply.

Poor Edwin! He was not given to violence, but had to give the lad a good tanning. Doug was always most surprised and aggrieved when taken to task. With Edwin gone Nancy knew that she could never control the boy.

His schooling had been almost completely ineffective. Although he enjoyed reading as he grew older, he could not spell the simplest words correctly. He became an excellent mimic of his teachers and especially of the saintly old man in Sunday School, who gallantly undertook to teach the boy his trade of shoe-making. It was useless, and the two parted company after a few weeks.

By the time he was seventeen Doug was seized with the idea that Canada was the place for him. He was sure he would make a farmer. He loved animals, (but not enough to tend any of Edwin's regularly) he loved the countryside and he wanted to travel.

Annie Meredith had wanted to travel, Nancy recalled. Perhaps among men in a man's world he would settle and begin to work. She scraped together the necessary money, fitted him out with clothes and saw him off with a mixture of relief and anxiety. During his four years away she received about four misspelt letters, and she knew that Dougie abroad had not changed. His first letter indicated that his boss was not paying him, and he complained of the harsh conditions. His mother's sympathies were divided equally between her lonely, rebellious son and any stranger trying to make the boy really work for his living. However, things improved when he was taken on by a kindly couple with an only son. They were glad of young company for their lad, and treated Doug generously. A letter from them to Nancy reassured her that he was indeed being treated as a second son and beginning to help willingly on the land. A later letter caused more concern, when it recounted a serious fall from a horse and three days' concussion. Always a dare-devil, but with no experience of handling a horse, Doug had insisted on trying his hand at breaking one in. He was never able to recall exactly what happened.

His twenty-first birthday drew near, and a hint that he might return to England was not followed by any definite news. Nancy was filled with very mixed feelings. She knew that his coming would increase her problems and wondered how he would pay for his passage home if his old bone-idleness had persuaded his friends in Winnipeg to suggest his leaving them.

In December she took his photograph to a local cinema, where a clairvoyant was claiming to give news of anyone whose photograph was held by her assistant. For some seconds the woman on the stage seemed to be groping, then she said, 'This young man is a very long way away, but he is returning. He will be with you again very early in the new year.' Doug did, in fact, walk in on New Year's Day. Bigger, stronger, with a decided Canadian accent and no small amount of swagger, but with a terrible tale to tell of how he had worked his passage home on a cattle boat.

His old cronies flocked round to hear all his stories. They were fascinated, and he an excellent raconteur. Shortly afterwards the eldest son of a local widow broke his mother's heart by insisting on going to Canada himself. He married a Red Indian girl and never returned.

It was always Doug's boast that the girl he married wasn't born yet, and her mother was dead, but that didn't stop the girls from chasing him, even the most eligible in the town. Outside the home he was vastly popular. Inside, his presence was still a torment to Nancy, especially as he had begun to drink by this time.

I remember very clearly the incident in the Gaiety cinema, when Mother took the snap of Doug. I was with her, and felt the electric atmosphere when the clairvoyant spoke. I remember also some time later arguing very hotly with a Methodist minister that some people had the powers of extrasensory perception – although I was too young to use that term. Mother's knowledge of Mary's death before she was told, and the fact that she always announced, 'I've been thinking a lot of Alf today – there'll be a letter tomorrow,' the day before a letter arrived, certainly impressed me. No doubt because of this my mind is very easy to 'tune in' to, for fortune tellers at garden fêtes and so on always tell me a great deal of the truth and forecast very accurately.

If you are wondering where I came into the story, I am the second Nancy – born in the middle of the war of a very weary mother, and having no real memory of the father I was said to resemble a great deal.

The rest of the family up to my birth had been born fair, but turned dark very early. Althea Edwina was born a tiny gypsy like her mother, and stayed dark. I was born fair and had a golden mop until my teens, when it darkened to light brown. Mendel would have been thrilled to see his theory so perfectly demonstrated. My mother stroked my hair hopefully and swore that it was 'turning' – willing it to go auburn like my father's. She was extremely jealous that her sister Fran had a red-headed daughter a year before I was born and her brother Joe a flaming red-head shortly after my birth.

But of course I did not remember my father, who died five days after Althea's birth and before I was two. For me Tom was always head of the family, and a dearer eldest brother no one ever had. I never knew him to do or say a mean or unkind thing. His health was never robust, but he did all he could, and enjoyed the love and friendship of many people. He won a scholarship to the nearest grammar school, but was turned down because of his dicky heart. He would have made a good schoolmaster, but he ended as representative for a Nottingham firm and he had friends in every village in North Nottinghamshire.

His main interest was music, and he had enough piano lessons to become an excellent sight reader and a popular accompanist at concerts. Some lessons developed his very pleasing baritone voice and he took part in the local amateur operatic productions for many years – loving every minute of it. He conducted and played for small male-voice choirs in some of the villages he knew and for us at home he was the great I AM in our joint family efforts.

As a little girl I stood on one footstool at the side of the old rosewood piano and Althea Edwina on the other. Tom played away, Alf with a beautiful tenor voice sang in the background, Denys later played the violin and Eric banged away on his wonderful collection of drums and home-made percussion instruments. A beautiful Indian brass vase was clanged from time to time, and the cymbals he operated with his feet. Doug, if at home, entered in with gusto and 'rawped'. His voice was never diagnosed as tenor or bass but was often used to give a moving rendering of 'Down in our garden suburb'. This ditty, with its 'far from the noise and hubbarb' he sang fortissimo and was always the end of any loftier musical aspirations. It always moved my mother out of the room.

The neighbours were apt to look in when they heard the din and the door was always open to any who wanted to join the fun. When Tom was not there and my cronies came round we would put on the gramophone, turn back the carpet and dance.

As my father's workshop had been a social centre I suppose our very ordinary home was one. In spite of her big brood my mother had always room in her heart for other children, and they always found her. The wealthiest family in the district had a huge house with big grounds and their own swimming pool. There were five or six headstrong, nanny-bullying handsome children there, but their mother was too busy entertaining or visiting her family in America to control the children. A long succession of nannies, and the cook and maids did their best, but achieved little. The youngest daughter used to leave them all and come to my mother for a bit of real mothering. At the other extreme the poor mentally deficient child of an incestuous union was always turning up and finding some kindness and comfort.

Mother's closest friend in the neighbourhood was the wife of a wholesale and retail fruiterer. They had built two substantial houses just after the row of smaller houses had been built across the road. Maria Foster had lost her third child, and never had a daughter. When tiny Althea was born she had eyed her covetously and said, 'A little gypsy at last.' Very dark herself, she was in fact to become mother to the frail little girl.

At four I had pneumonia and was very ill. I'm sorry to say one of my earliest memories is of the battle of wills over taking medicine. The grim-faced old doctor wouldn't accept mother's announcement that I wouldn't take the bitter stuff. He got Tom and my mother to hold me and force my mouth open and he showed how he could put it in. Disgusting child that I was, I waited for them to let go and then spat it in the doctor's face. When I pulled round the doctor said my mother must get away for a holiday and try to leave little Althea where she could be well cared for.

Maria Foster leapt at the chance of getting the little girl into her comfortable home, and mother took me to stay with her elder brother and his wife and son. I remember Cousin Tom's wonderful collection of butterflies. He'd had one little sister who had died and he made a great fuss of me. At bed time I kept calling from my room, 'Goodnight Tom,' and revelled in hearing his, 'Goodnight, Nancy,' over and over again.

When we went back home Maria begged to keep Althea a bit longer whilst mother's health improved. The 'bit longer' in fact stretched to a lifetime. Our home was a rowdy, boy-ridden establishment, Claremont, the Foster home, was a haven of comfort and plenty; but alas for Althea, Maria's very real love of her never compensated for being away from her own mother. She was always running across the road for a love from 'Mamma', as she called her, and wanting to join in my tomboyish pursuits.

CHAPTER THREE

CHILDHOOD

We were very lucky in our childhood background. Apart from Claremont and the neighbouring house we had nothing but fields across the road. The last lamp in the street faced our front bedroom window and must have attracted the moths from the wood and hedges. On the whole I was a fearless child, but when the big moths came into the bedroom I was terrified. Two houses away on our side of the road was the Little Wood. It was our main playground in the day time. Rival gangs made huts of branches and uttered fearful threats to anyone who approached. Mere girls were never allowed inside. Coarse and terrible were the epithets hurled at anyone from a rival gang. There was a tree called the Cradle where the boys could hide without being seen through the thick foliage. I was terribly envious of them. No climber was I, but a great acrobat on the lowest branch of a big beech we called the Cherry Tree. I've no idea why it was so called.

One day when alone I determined to climb the Cherry Tree. It was very difficult and I scraped myself badly, but I made fast progress. My chagrin was great when I found that for the life of me I couldn't get down again. It was at the far end of the wood from the houses and I had to wait until my mother came to seek me. A ladder was borrowed from a building site behind the wood and I wobbled down very thankfully.

We knew all the farms for some distance round, and I went with Denys carrying the milk can if we needed more milk in the evening. It was a great thrill to go up the lanes and along cart tracks on a winter's evening with stars coming out. We were sometimes allowed to see the calves and let them suck our fingers with their rough strong tongues. We loved the old gentle sheepdog at one of the farms and wept when she was put to sleep at the ripe old age of twenty-one!

Family group 1930, author second from left, front, aged 13.

The builders gradually filled in all the road with houses and some of the farm houses are now difficult to pick out amongst the modern homes all round. As I pass now I remember my picnics with Eileenan' Audrey, my bosom friends. The thrill of sitting under hawthorn bushes snowy white with may, of finding a beautiful fairy ring in one of Farmer Cullen's fields, and the annual event of picking big bunches of moonpennies and trembling grass were all shared with Eileenan' Audrey, who lived in a much bigger family than ours next door but one.

They were not allowed to go on the really long expeditions when I went with Denys and older children for a day's outing to Lindrick Dale. It was a very long walk along the Sheffield road, and we always stopped to refresh ourselves with pop and sweets at the tiny toll-bar shop half way. We crossed the golf course and found the spring which trickled into the stream near 'brick bottom'. We then paddled our tired feet in the cold water there under the bushes. Perhaps it had once been a mill race. We followed the stream towards the Dale and there explored the very exciting caves. A ford, another spring, a steep grassy slope you could roll down were our attractions there, and a boggy wood full of stinking nannies ran along by the lane back to the main road. The long trek back home was a great anti-climax. On one occasion Althea wheedled permission to come with us to Lindrick, and had to be 'pagged' home. This meant taking it in turns to carry her on our backs – an extremely wearisome business at the end of a long day.

The last time I visited Lindrick Dale our childhood paradise had been blasted to bits and quarrying was going on all round. The Little Wood, Moonpenny Field and Fairy Ring Meadow are all now incorporated in the gardens of the houses built since I was very young. However, the lovely big woods are still there further out in the country and I could show where we found scarlet pimpernels and foxgloves near Peak's Hill. I expect if we followed the path round there would still be a spring and water cress and golden water blobs in the field near Owday Lane. I like to think so.

When I was almost seven my mother was knocked down by a lorry. Buses had begun to run every half hour into the town, and for mother the weekly choir practice held in the Methodist Church was a 'must'. The doctor had insisted that whatever else went by the board she must keep up her singing, and this meant a desperate skiffle round in order to get there on time. Her legs were in a terrible state and the double journey was more than she could face at the end of a busy day. Alas, her eye was on the bus coming in from the country and she didn't see the lorry bowling out from the town. Her leg was broken and she was taken to hospital and suddenly we were without father and mother. Althea was still with the Fosters, Denys was fetched by Aunt Allie from Goosnargh, near Preston, and I was taken first to one relation and then to a cousin of my father's.

They made a great fuss of me, and my prodigious appetite for such a skinny child was a wonder to them all. My boy cousin, Alan, was away at college, but came home for Christmas whilst I was there. Used as I was to being considered a 'mere' girl in a household of boys I found it hard to believe that my big handsome cousin considered me worthy of his attention. It was my seventh birthday whilst I was there and Aunt Allie sent me a beautiful blue satin party dress with pink roses round the neck and waist. I'd never had such a truly splendid garment. Kind friends from the Methodist Church lived near the school I had to attend and they had me in for my midday meals. Winifred, their only child, was my bosom friend at Sunday school and she also attended the day school. My blue party frock was copied in pink by her mother and fine bows of ribbon to match adorned our heads as we went off proudly to the school Christmas party. Winifred wanted to know which of us looked prettier. Her poor mother was in a dilemma. I knew the blue suited my golden curls and grey-blue eyes, but Winifred was not so skinny, and filled out her dress nicely. In the end her diplomatic mother decided I was prettier but Winifred bonnier.

For Christmas, which my poor mother spent very painfully in hospital, I was given two dressing up cardboard dolls, one dark, one fair, and sets of clothes to hang on them. I thought dark straight hair was very enviable, but Alan criticised me for giving the prettiest dresses to the dark doll. He insisted that the other deserved them because she was like me. In fact my curly hair was the bane of my life. I was always flying about, and it was never tidy. Brushing and combing it was an ordeal I hated.

Alan's younger sister Ada, aged about seventeen, loved brushing and combing my hair. One day when my aunt was out she decided to bring me up to date and cut a fringe. Fringes and curly hair don't go easily together and the harder Ada tried to get it straight the shorter my fringe became. By the time my aunt returned it was little more than an elevated skew-wiff, moustache, and poor Ada was reduced to tears for taking such liberties. After that my mother was consulted and I was taken to a barber to be 'put right', and indeed properly bobbed. What a relief! My hair was much less of a problem after that.

In hospital things were going badly. The broken leg had to be re-set and mother was in for ten weeks. The bigger boys had been left at home to cope by themselves with 'poor Annie Berry' coming in to cook a mid-day meal. Poor Annie had been born of a middle-aged man and his ailing wife, and was motherless from infancy. The culinary arts had not been taught her and the boys complained bitterly of the atrocious meals she served up. The 'pièce de résistance' was a rice pudding cooked in the frying pan.

The girl and her father were two of the people mother tried to help, in spite of all her own difficulties. As later on people used to bring stray animals to me, any people in difficulty were introduced to my mother. In this way she was put on by many who knew her good nature and wanted to be rid of encumbrances or expense.

At one time a relation from abroad arrived with four children and a foreign maid, and the 'night or two' extended until we were desperate. Mother was incapable of turning anyone away. A French woman and her daughter were wished on us 'temporarily' and again they settled far too long for our comfort. The daughter had all the wiles of an attractive French teenager and my older brothers were at the age when flirting was a great game. Mother thought the situation was fraught with danger and they eventually moved on.

The longest invasion was by an old man who had quarrelled with his son and decided to return and beg a permanent home with his old neighbour. Alf was at the house when he arrived and was told they just hadn't room for him. The old man said nothing on earth would make him go back to his son, and Alf said, 'Come home with me, we'll put you up for the night.'

That was it. We had him for months, and he tried to rule our house with a rod of iron, as no doubt he'd tried to rule his son's and been shown the door. Denys and I weren't used to such a grim face and bad temper, and we would have fits of the giggles which nearly drove him mad. His health declined, and mother put him a bed in our sitting-room and nursed him for weeks. We called him Granddad Otter, as we'd never any real granddads to remember. In his softer moods I think he knew that he was very fortunate to have finished in the hands of my good-natured mother. He left her £20 in his will and bought me my first watch for my eighth birthday. He also gave me my first cat – a Manx, completely wild, which he begged from Farmer Cullen.

I called her Brownie and gradually tamed her. She was just beginning to accept our friendship when a ginger tom arrived from nowhere. He terrified poor Brownie, and she bolted down the cellar and hid behind the coal. By the time we'd clambered over to her she was always somewhere else, and we could not persuade her to come up the steps. I took food down to her and left it in the part where we stored our apples and potatoes. Gradually I put food on the steps, higher and higher until she was eating at the top. She ventured into the living room at last, but on her first step outside the wretched tom appeared again. Brownie shot away, and I thought I'd lost her. I left food in the yard, it was always gone by morning and one day she emerged from under the raised floor of the henhouse with two little balls of fluff wobbling after her. They had little stumps for tails. One was ginger and the other the most beautiful tortoiseshell. Ginger was begged by Eileen an' Audrey and I kept Topsy, who was my dear delight for several years and the inspiration of my first song.

I composed the song whilst having a bath in the draughty North-facing bathroom at Claremont. It was in cat language and went as follows:

Verse 1   Rue har a nitha puthy
             Rue har a nitha tatt
             Rue har a nitha puthy
             Ath boo'ful ath my hat

Rue har a nitha puthy
Rue'th got a pretty nothe
And altho now I come to look
Rue'th got thum pretty toeth.

Verse 2   My kittenth name ith Topthy
Itth quite a pretty name
And if you do not like it
You can lump it – all the thame
Thee'th only quite a kitten
You can't call her a cat
And ath I have before mentioned
Thee'th boo'ful ath my hat.

The tune was original with overtones of Charlie Parker's banjo ditties.

Denys and Althea hated the song. They went frantic when I addressed Topsy in 'cat language' but I consoled myself by the knowledge that they'd never composed a song in any language. Charlie Parker was a maker of bicycles and a bit of a card. He was a member of the Methodist choir and a friend of mine from as early as I was able to sit through an evening service without making too much fuss. The tenors sat behind the sopranos and when my fidgets were almost beyond control I would feel a tap on my shoulder and a very hot peppermint lozenge would be slid surreptitiously down the seat into my hand. My eyes streamed and I gasped for breath as I sucked away, very conscious of the honour.

When we had a concert Charlie was always there, and he and Alf sang risqué duets – to the chagrin of the more straight-laced of the church members and the embarrassment of my poor mother. However, they were both born entertainers and helped the concerts to go with a swing, and indeed the words of the songs wouldn't raise half an eyebrow now. Another 'regular' at the concerts was Sam Hardisty. He was Yorkshire born and bred and gave readings in Yorkshire dialect. He had a marvellous sense of timing and a very jolly red face and was greatly appreciated. Duets were sung by our leading bass, an enormous dignified gentleman – a pourer of

28

oil on troubled waters and a plumber by profession – and a tiny tenor who sang everything with his mouth in a tight little 'o', and always looked as if he would go pop at any moment. My musical sense was overcome by my sense of humour. They made such a comical pair that I had to laugh, however movingly they sang, 'O who will o'er the downs so free?'

Mother installed a bath in the kitchen, but my earliest memories include baths taken in front of a roaring fire, in rain water. Our rain water tub was an outsize, as the tap water was very hard, and it was a 'must' to heat rain water for hair washing and washing woollen garments. When I was out of the bath and my hair being rubbed dry I sat on my mother's knee and she sang ad infinitum. It never occurred to me that Althea was missing so much at Claremont.

After my father's death I shared the big bed with my mother and this probably added to my sense of security. Denys would come creeping in on the other side of Mother for a love in the early morning. I thought it was very babyish of him, being a very independent child and tired of hearing, 'Lie still and don't kick my legs!' As she had thirteen ulcers on the leg she didn't break, it was no wonder that I had to try to lie still. It was the most difficult thing for me to keep still, and that, coupled with my skinny frame and enormous appetite made her shake her head sadly and say, 'I'm sure that child's got worms.'

After leaving Infants'School my earliest friendships began to crumble. Eileenan' Audrey went to a church school and we as a family continued our education in the ex-Methodist school in the town. Almost two miles away, it meant a great deal of walking, indeed running, at midday, as there were no facilities for meals there. The only concession for those of us from outside the town was permission to take food and eat it by Miss Vaines' fire in very snowy weather.

Miss Vaines had the 'duffers' class, and seemed to enjoy it. Her numbers were relatively small and the choicest of the bricks they dropped she would come and relate to my teacher, roaring with laughter. I say 'my teacher' because the two years I spent in her class were an eternity to me. She was the stage type of bad-tempered spinster schoolmarm, convinced that the more strict she was, the more we would take in. Her snappy manner had

1933 – author first left, back row – Upper VA.

the reverse effect on me, and I was kept in to learn the names of the rivers of England and sent back every time I joined the knitting queue to 'do it again!' 'It' was the heel of a sock and Snappy So-and-So sent me back without glancing at my miserable efforts as often as not. I swore to myself I'd never knit another sock as long as I lived.

It was different when the headmaster came in. My brain cleared and I understood and could answer all his questions. He was our new head, and very popular after the iron rule of his unimaginative predecessor.

The latter had gone to be head of a new secondary school and Denys was still suffering under him. When his glasses were broken and left with the head to be sent for repairs Denys went several times to see if they were back, and was always told, 'Not yet.' He couldn't see the blackboard and was getting very much behind with his work when Mother made bold to go and see what had happened. Again the head said he couldn't help the delay. They weren't back yet. Mother spotted the case amongst piles of things on his desk and said, 'What are these?' It was the glasses which had not yet been sent away. She was hopping mad. I heard the tale and decided nothing would get me to *that* school.

One winter's dinner time I was wandering about the cloakroom filling in time when a monitor came along. We were alone, but she said, 'Walk on your toes in the cloakroom,' stalking round on her own heels to annoy me.

I said, 'I will when you do.'

'I'll tell Snappy So-and-So,' she retorted and went off to do so.

I was flabbergasted when Snappy appeared and ticked me off for not obeying a monitor and keeping the rule of 'walking on toes'. I burst into uncontrollable sobs at such injustice, and poor Snappy became alarmed. To my increasing chagrin she put me on her knee and tried to comfort me. Miss Vaines was there and the two tried to talk me round.

'Are you going with Denys to the Secondary School when you leave?' they asked.

I burst out, 'No, and Denys hates it and I'm not going there!'

This remark was repeated by Snappy to the old head, who had Denys up in front of the whole school and read him a sermon on loyalty.

My future was settled in the end by the new head, who dropped the remark one day that it was a pity I wasn't doing homework and preparing for the scholarship exam for the High School eight miles away. It was my chance and I took it. Mother was staggered when I went home and said I had told the head I wanted to join the scholarship group. I joined them rather late and didn't get a full scholarship, but I did get a free place which meant no fees, although books and fares were a considerable item to my mother.

The High School, a smart uniform, train-rides, a well-equipped gymnasium, an English mistress who read poetry so that I went home and memorized reams in no time – all heaven after two long years in Snappy's class. After my first day I ran across to Althea at Claremont and sang the songs we'd been taught and told her all the delights.

It was a foregone conclusion that Althea would go into the scholarship group as soon as possible and follow me to the High School. A holy hush surrounded her homework sessions – very different from the noise and ragging going on round me – and she got in with a full scholarship the next September. She was a quiet, well-behaved child and made steady progress. I enjoyed every minute of life and worked just enough to 'get by'. If Althea couldn't understand her maths she wept in despair. If I couldn't understand mine I took it that Kiltie hadn't made it very clear and if my poor marks encouraged her to explain it again I was doing everybody a good turn.

As a class I disliked English French mistresses. They made gruesome faces and horrible noises, and French verbs were 'barmy'. When the headmistress imported a real live Frenchwoman I warmed to her. She spoke English littered with French and I spoke French littered with English. It was virtually the same language. Her accent was the same as the Madame my poor Mamma had been 'landed with' some time earlier. When she heard that my father's family had been French she became very excited. Alas, she was ragged most pitilessly by the form as a whole, and when the two prize gigglers were on form she would cry in despair, 'Wi' you stop zeese geegling?' adding her mangled version of the names of the offenders. It was fuel to the fire, and the whole form would join in. In summer we would pretend to be gasping for air and beg to have our conversation lessons out on the field under the trees. Mademoiselle Marie Antoinette de

Noirefontaine was as keen for a diversion as we were, and she would go across to her flat for the wonderful raffia-embroidered straw hat which she felt necessary to wear in the sun. She then emerged like a ship in full sail and we followed like a gaggle of geese and sought every possible delay before settling down. The bell for the next lesson usually rang before we'd finished seeing spiders in each other's hair.

Her reign was short, but we learnt some songs and put on a revue-cum-*thé dansant* called *Moulin Blanc* before she left. I was dragooned into singing the solos and acting the part of a stupid French girl. I still remember every word, and my rude mocking of the English Frenchmistress, Miss B, who presumed to interfere and polish up my enunciation. I popped my eyes out like hers, and did an exaggerated copy a few inches from her nose. It raised a gasp and a laugh from the onlookers, and I was then left in peace – odious child that I was. Most of the form cheated in *dictées* taken by the English Frenchmistress. It was beneath my dignity, and my marks were shocking. However, for the School Certificate exam, we had a real Frenchman and I came top with another none-too-brilliant pupil. Miss B was furious. 'You do very badly for me every week and then come out top in the Concours. I wash my hands of you!' Nothing could have suited me better.

We were promised that we could choose our subjects in the sixth form, but we were short of staff and obliged to take what fitted in with the mistresses available. This meant French again and Maths. I was not very pleased, but I made the most of English, which I adored, and Biology – a new subject in the school. None of us passed in Biology. The mistress never discovered what we ought to be learning, but she waxed most interesting on her own pet subject and although I boggled at dissection I found the lessons as a whole very absorbing.

During my last years at school I was granted an Intermediate scholarship for intending teachers. There were not many careers open to girls in those days and my mother often said, 'If you've any sense you'll train as a teacher and not run the risk of being left as I was with a houseful of kids and no means of earning a living. You could be a headmistress like Miss Sykes with a house to yourself and a little maid to wait on you hand and foot.' I don't know whether Miss Sykes' ears burned. I never really aspired to being so exalted.

By this time all the older boys but Doug were married, and I was an aunt in a big way. I was used to young children and enjoyed handling them. The nearest school was the Infants' School I'd attended myself and I went there to observe for a few weeks each year. The High School holidays were much longer, and this system of observing was an essential part of the training in our county.

It was a happy school, very efficiently run by a tiny frail woman. I got to know the staff there and asked if I might do my pre-college years there. This followed the year after I was eighteen, and was also part of the county's scheme for preparing pupils for teaching. We were called Young Persons in Training, and we spent half our time in the schools and half attached to the local Technical College. There we had courses in music, handwork, needlework, elocution, physical education and so on. We made posters and had to produce drawings and do a fantastic amount of work at home to keep up with everything. When teachers were ill we found ourselves in charge of classes and we were obliged to prepare and give criticism lessons which the headmistress attended. It was hard work, but very useful. Just how useful I didn't appreciate until I reached College.

Just before leaving for College I was invited to spend a holiday in Yorkshire at the house where Doug was in digs. In his way he was very fond of his family and proud of them, too, I think. He had given me my first bicycle – a ramshackle affair called Esmeralda. She was very ancient and sometimes needed a good kick. As a mere girl I was expected to wait on my brothers hand and foot, and Doug in particular never lifted a finger in the home. When he arrived home, however, he always had a caseful of home made cakes and a bird from his landlady, and I looked forward to meeting her. Her husband was the village blacksmith – a large, silent man. Mrs S was small and dark – a vivacious woman, fond of company and resentful of the hard life she lived in the remote village. Her firstborn was slightly deformed, but I believe an intelligent boy. The younger boy was rough and tough and only five when I went there.

Doug was a born teaser and ragged the boys until they were angry. When this happened young Robert would begin to swear like a trooper. On one such occasion I told him that if he used such bad language I'd wash his mouth out with carbolic soap. There ensued a further stream of foul epithets and I grabbed him, took him into the kitchen and fulfilled my threat.

When he'd finished spitting and spluttering he rounded on me, 'Thoo, Thoo, Tha's nobbut a lidle skealtaicher!' It cut me down to size, and I never forgot his remark. When I find myself getting too uppity I remind myself of what Robert said. Five year olds are very sagacious, and rarely treated as such.

When I was in my teens Bank Holidays were one long slog at home. Doug's arrival always caused a great stir. The older boys in the neighbours' families came to see him. The gramophone was playing by the hour. Although Doug never attempted to play an instrument, he collected good recordings of the popular shows, and *Showboat, Mr Cinders, No No Nanette* and so on were played repeatedly. Paul Robeson was a favourite, too. I was expected to dance attendance and provide some sort of refreshments for all the gang. Women's Lib. was undreamt of in those days, and if I jibbed at being on the run all the time I was scolded for being awkward. I was prevailed upon to peel potatoes and make chips in an old frying pan when all else failed. I did this over an open fire and roasted myself purple before I'd satisfied their rapacious appetites; but they gobbled them appreciatively, called me a good cook, and I saw myself more in the light of queen of the back parlour than unpaid skivvy.

In addition to helping prepare all the food at Christmas and doing all the marketing it fell to my lot to do all Doug's shopping as well. My own modest presents were often made for the growing number of nieces and bought for the other members of the family in good time, but on Christmas Eve I was cajoled into accepting a pocketful of money (Doug's pockets were never empty!) and fighting my way round the shops on Doug's behalf. My Christmas charity waxed very threadbare by the time I'd selected all the things I couldn't afford, but knew Doug could. It is almost unbelievable, but when I reached home late and exhausted I was fool enough to wrap them up for him, too.

On Christmas Day he would put on a modest air when people said, 'Oh, how generous! Really Doug you shouldn't!' He would then say, 'Oh well, Nance chose it. I'm not much good at that sort of thing.' The trouble with me was that I was very good at that sort of thing, and always knew what people would like, and indeed couldn't resist facing the crowds and the dark wet streets and queuing for treasures. As his instructions always included, 'And get something for yourself,' it was hard to refuse. There were no shops in the village where he lived and his contacts with the nearest town were almost entirely connected with his fondness for beer-drinking.

As a similar tendency had ruined the life of her youngest brother my mother was vehement in her loathing of beer. I must admit that the smell of it is nauseating to me, and when Doug took me to visit a great friend of his, the landlady of a pub he frequented, I expected to see the very embodiment of all that is fast and destructive. She was in fact a sweet, gentle woman and greeted me graciously. I gathered that Doug helped her put her gross besotted spouse to bed when he had trouble in getting up the stairs. Doug was very sorry for her, but saw no danger in his own increasing fondness for alcohol.

CHAPTER FOUR

POTTER STREET AND PUBERTY

Until I left for College almost all my social life was centred round the Methodist Church, where my parents were married and all of us christened. We always called it Potter Street, after its location.

The early death of my father, and her many family obligations made it difficult for my mother to keep up with all the activities there, but unless she was ill she never missed the Sunday evening service and the choir practice. When she had the energy she would attend the Monday afternoon women's meeting. I went with her on many occasions and I remember hearing and fully understanding a talk on 'The second mile'. Certainly as a family we were always encouraged to go the second mile with anyone, and if our own affairs suffered thereby we made many friends. Mother had little enough, but anything in the nature of a windfall she always shared with someone less fortunate.

At harvest festivals we trailed into town laden with fruit, flowers and vegetables. When he was old enough, Eric took on one of the extra plots my father had used for providing for us during the war. He worked very hard all day and then spent every available minute cherishing his flowers and vegetables. He was a very good son. The scarlet fever he had miraculously survived left him with impaired hearing and a very husky voice, but that didn't prevent him from making joyful, if rather gruesome, 'music' when he was working.

When Eric married he kept on the extra garden, but the one at home went downhill rapidly. In the end I took it on myself with some help and advice from a neighbour. It was very exciting to produce fantastically big cabbages on the plot where there had been hens and ducks when we were children. Denys helped to lay a lawn where mother had had her roses and herb garden, and interested friends helped me to make a rockery.

Having attended the evening service with mother since a very young child I automatically joined the choir when I reached my teens. The choir practice was held most conveniently on the same night, but an hour later than the Young People's Class meeting. All my closest friends at church attended both. Methodism meant singing, and we all had enough music lessons to be able to sight-read and play the piano. Some were very good musicians and the choir practice was the highlight of the week.

When we were short of contraltos I joined Winifred and Dorothy Hardisty (the daughter of Sam the Yorkshire man, and an excellent musician) and a dear Beatrix Potter – style little lady, who wobbled uncertainly on the lower notes. Normally I sang soprano, which was really more my range, but swapping about was good for sightreading. Our regular organist was a 'bit of a lad' and a great enthusiast. When we first went through the *Messiah* he nearly died with laughing at our effort at sight-reading 'All we like sheep.' His eyes streamed with tears and he all but fell from his perch in front of the organ. But we mastered every note in every run before we put it on, and the church was absolutely packed, with people sitting on the stairs. The mayor opened the proceedings and we had excellent soloists from Sheffield. We took £5 in collections, which was a fabulous sum to our little church in those days.

Social evenings were put on every few months or so in the winter. The teenage group used to meet once a week and practise playlets, or sketches. This was great fun, and we always had a play up our sleeves if anyone wanted to put an extra item in a concert. During one of these concerts we put on a school play and I wore my school uniform. Whilst we were having refreshments afterwards the 'young' minister (we always had a 'young' unmarried minister attached to the circuit) came to me and said, 'Take off those terrible clothes. You look about fifteen!' I replied, 'I am fifteen.' He coloured up and turned away, and I realized that my very warm feelings for him were returned, but having seen me only in my Sunday best he thought I was much nearer his own age. His smiles didn't come my way so often after that, and I was heartbroken when I knew that a certain matron in the church invited him to tea always when he was preaching at our services. Inevitably he walked to church with her vivacious daughter and I was very jealous.

At one concert about the same time Althea and I were prevailed upon to sing a duet. Although we both sang in the choir it was a very different thing to sing on our own. We were both petrified. Very unwisely we decided to sing an old canon we'd learnt at school – 'Clouds o'er the summer sky'. When nervous, Althea always sought refuge in speed, and she began at a rattling pace. I began my part three notes later and we blushed and trilled our way nervously to a hasty conclusion. I regret to say that a bunch of visiting scouts at the back of the room took it that my starting the same tune after Althea was all a big mistake. By the time we'd finished, their sniggers had progressed through stifled laughter to unchecked roars of merriment. I had always thought scouts in numbers to be a lewd and ignorant mob. By the end I think they had decided it was supposed to be a comic turn and they clapped loud applause. Althea and I were not amused. We never sang a duet in public again.

Although mother sang so effortlessly in public, as did all her family, we inherited a streak from my father's family which made it very difficult. I was not afflicted in the same way over speaking, reciting and acting, and at the age of fifteen I was producing plays and acting in them both at school and in the church. At that time my memory was fantastic and I was often able to prompt all the others without a copy. Alf had inherited the same gift from my father and he could hold an audience spellbound. His diction was clear, his voice musical and every word beautifully balanced. It was a pity that he did not make acting his career, but it was a family tradition that gifts were for giving away, not for 'exploiting for filthy lucre!' Throughout his life he's never been well off financially, but he's given endless hours of pleasure and made innumerable friends.

At fifteen I was a full-blooded adolescent, but nobody took the trouble to explain why I had changed from a lively, friendly child into an awkward rebel. Nothing and nobody could really please me. Mother found me very trying and my impudence very exasperating. Her only attempt at violence towards me was landing out with the dishcloth when my tongue was particularly vixenish one day. I was appalled. I don't remember ever being slapped, which I'm sure I must have deserved often enough. Having accepted with Doug that 'if you knocked one devil out you knocked two more in' she was much too lenient with us. As Denys had gone through the 'awkward stage' with every excuse made for taciturnity and small outbursts of rebellion, I fired out one day, 'Denys was allowed to have an awkward stage, but I'm not!'

Even my closest school friend seemed like an alien to me at that time, and school itself I began to loathe. During the winter preceding my sitting for School Certificate I took it upon myself to enlarge my sphere and learn shorthand and typing at night school. This meant two more nights out each week, and I was already spending more time than my standard of attainment justified in extra-school activities. Mother's leniency was no doubt partly to blame, and apart from English I was not giving nearly enough time to my homework. The Maths mistress would listen incredulously to my proving of theorems and say at the end, 'Well you've got there, Nancy, but how on airth I don't know. It's not in the book.' In one Maths exam I staggered myself by coming out top, with a very high mark. The same little Scottish lady said of my result that no one was more surprised than she. She was mistaken! I was bottom in Algebra about the same time. Most people were terrified of her. I was not, and never pretended to understand when I did not. Several of the form always worked together to flog out difficult problems. When I worked I worked alone, but I didn't tear my hair out if I couldn't see the light.

My school friends included several from small villages and one from an isolated farm. Visits to them were made to coincide with dances in the winter or garden fêtes in the summer. It was an interesting experience to grope one's way down ice-packed, deeply-rutted lanes by the light of a lantern. The village or school hall was always crowded, and the temperature varied from ice-cold by the door to roasting hot by the stove at the other end of the room. At the whist drive preceding one dance I won the ladies' prize – a pair of thick, fleecy-lined slippers. On our way to catch the bus the following Monday morning we met an old man who had been playing. He eyed me balefully and said his old woman could have done with 'them slippers'. I felt very mean to be taking them out of the village without realising how much they were valued in another quarter.

My first visit in Spring coincided with more cock crowing and cow mooing than I had thought possible in one place. A bit later the animal noises were joined by most unearthly shrieks from the orchard. My friend thought me an awful townie and explained that a child came to 'tent' the cherries. This meant dashing hither and thither and making as much noise as possible to keep the birds off. In addition to rattling things she made a noise like a banshee. I believe she received three pence a day for her efforts. It was well-earned. I decided that 'a quiet country life' was a myth. It was much quieter in our home on the outskirts of a small town.

That is not to say that I didn't love staying there, even when water on the wash-stand had ice on it in the mornings and the fire lit in the bedroom to keep us warm was of purely decorative value, as the sky could be seen up the chimney, and any heat from the logs went straight up there. We lit log fires, very smoky, in a little room called the Den downstairs, and ate mountains of apples and read old 'Strand' magazines by the hour.

At strawberry and raspberry time we had freshly-gathered fruit with cream at every meal. Happy memories!

The one thing I couldn't stand was drinking rain water. It ran off the roof to a big tank underground and was pumped up into the kitchen. By the end of the summer it was distinctly 'high', and a dark colour. My friend assured me that it couldn't be poisonous, as people in their village often lived to be over ninety. I answered that no self-respecting germ could have survived in such water, and poured as much concentrated fruit juice in as possible.

On her return visits my friend shook us by asking if she might have a drink from our rain butt as the water from the taps had no flavour. No dead birds and rats could get into our tub, so no doubt our best didn't match up to what she had at home, for her brother assured me he'd taken both from their water tank at one time or another. He could have been pulling my leg, as a great deal of ragging went on, but from the colour and flavour I had no reason to doubt that he spoke the truth. Like his sister he was a voracious reader and would pick up one of my text books and devour it with great relish. 'Jolly interesting about so-and-so, isn't it, Nan?' he would say, as he

*A scene from the play, 'The Immortal Lady' by Clifford Bax
which I produced at College, May 1938.*

Trying on the costumes.

put the book down to select another apple or poke the smouldering logs on the fire. He carried off most of the prizes at school without seeming to work at all. I was green with envy.

No school prizes ever came my way, and yet I was expected to write poems for the magazine, produce plays, conduct the house choir and lead the house gymnastics team for the competitions. The latter two chores I suffered agonies over, but the swots would propose me and find every excuse for not being drawn in themselves. Writing poetry and producing plays I thoroughly enjoyed.

I became expert at just failing exams, the passing of which would have determined my further study of subjects I disliked. In this way, by two marks I left Latin behind and took up Domestic Science which I enjoyed, and thought would be of much greater use. In Chemistry my brinkmanship almost let me down. I failed by one mark only, and the mistress was very angry. I honestly wanted to study Botany, as I loved flowers and we were in an ideal area for getting specimens. When the mistress, who took both subjects, said to me, 'I'm disgusted with you, Nancy. If you don't do well in Botany I shall put you back on Chemistry and make you do extra lessons in the dinner hour,' I took heed. My interest in the flowers and trees was genuine, as was my loathing for the terrible feats of memory needed for Chemistry. In both cases it meant that I was choosing less 'scholarly' subjects, but I never considered myself a scholar – excepting in English, where I always came top.

I adored our tubby, twinkling-eyed English mistress. She was a trainer of the mind and not a crammer. She opened our eyes in all sorts of ways, and was one of the sanest people I've ever met. We remained friends until her death.

CHAPTER FIVE

COLLEGE

When the time came to apply for a place at College I was torn. My aunt, who was very keen that I should become a fully-qualified teacher, and had taken the greatest interest in us all since my father's death, wanted me to go to Ormskirk, which was near her home. Her only child had died many years earlier, and she would have loved to have me near enough to visit. I was at the stage of wanting to get right away from all family ties, and I'd set my heart on going to London, having been told that Avery Hill was excellent for kindergarten work. The aerial photograph of the College showing it in the middle of a park, with my beloved trees all round, was very attractive. I was told that if I applied to London at all I'd have to put it first and that any chances of getting in were slight, so I put Avery Hill at the top of the list and Ormskirk second. I got in, and so my whole future was determined.

At the interview for College I was questioned by the principal, who, unknown to me, was sister of a famous actor. She asked me why I wanted to teach, and I replied that I was fond of children. 'Isn't there anything else you would rather do?' she pressed. I admitted that I would really prefer to be an actress, but there wasn't much chance of that. She showed an amused interest. 'Well, why not. What are you doing here, then?' I said my mother was a widow and acting was a chancy business. She agreed that it was, and added, 'You might get the chance to work on the College play. There is one produced every year, you know.' I didn't know but I made a mental note and watched for my chances.

Another girl from my old school was also accepted at Avery Hill. Her mother was a widow, too, and the two of them saw us off on the train the September following our year as Young Persons in Training. They both looked forlorn standing by the little wicket gate, and I felt a tug at my heart as we waved goodbye. It was obvious that handkerchiefs would be out before our train had vanished. Eileen was an only child, and Mother had only Denys left of her big brood. He was very quiet, and after eating his evening meal he usually buried himself in a book. Mother was used to my chattering about the children and she liked to watch me doing the craft work and give a hand now and again. It was the end of an era, and she admitted at Christmas that she had been very lonely. She had taken to spoiling Richard, the cat, to compensate.

My aunt compensated for my not being near her by giving me the name and address of someone in London who had said that I might spend the odd weekend there. When I made a note of the details I little realized what the name and address would mean. Eventually both became mine.

Most of my memories of College are happy ones. Self-reliant by nature I was not among those who were in tears at being away from home. In any case I had spent holidays away from home on and off from the age of eleven, visiting relations or friends on my own. I was more deeply attached to my family and friends in the Methodist Church than I realized at the time, and as the weeks passed by I began to long to hear the lower and more pleasantly modulated voices of North Nottinghamshire. I liked the cheeky cock-sparrowness of the real Cockneys, and their warmth and friendliness, but their strident voices irritated after a few months.

The College was non-denominational, and for the first time I was rubbing shoulders with people from all over the country and of every denominational and political colour.

There was only one other active Methodist resident in our hall, and she was a most lovable and friendly soul. She sang like a nightingale, with no nerves at all, and was a great healer in any catty squabbles. We went together to the nearest Methodist Church and were warmly welcomed and invited to tea and biscuits after the evening service. We also went on our first outing into the big bad city together. We took parcels of hostel sandwiches (known as 'hostiles') and gave the excess of bread to the birds in the park. After that we did the sights, enquiring of the legendary London policemen where places were, and being treated most indulgently, even when we were swinging on railings to rest out feet. We visited Jerome's and had three postcard-size portraits each for sixpence halfpenny. I don't suppose the whole day cost more than half-a-crown each, for that would have been a very extravagant venture for either of us.

Before the first term was out I was proposed as Entertainments' Representative and found that I was expected to produce a play or some sort of variety show during the last week. We put on a crazy sketch for the benefit of the Warden and her deputy and all the older students. I dressed as a gawky young swain and lisped and stammered my way through a love scene, with the songbird Katie taking the part of my adored 'Thuson'. I still have the Jerome postcard portrait of Katie with, 'Luv Susan' written on the back. I had held the back to the audience whilst I made up excruciating verse to her. The Warden, who was an English lecturer, rolled with laughing and told me she thought I was making it up on the spot.

Alas, dear little Katie died very young of cancer. They say the good die young. I'm sure she never made an enemy in her life, though I remember her sitting in the middle of a long table waving a large carving knife and shouting, 'Anyone for another slice of bread?' above the din of hostel teatime. She looked very dangerous.

We ate far too much bread as our lives were lived to the full and the amount of protein we were allowed didn't keep us satisfied. We all grew very fat in the first term, and hoped that the senior students were right and that we should lose it quickly enough when we became embroiled in school practice later in the year.

Our curriculum was determined largely by the age group of the children we were likely to teach. I was enrolled for the kindergarten course which covered infants and lower juniors. In addition to Method, Music, Handwork, Physical Training, Biology, Social History and so on we were all obliged to take Psychology to Advanced level. Apart from these studies we all took another Advanced subject of our own choosing – not related to our course necessarily. As I had always enjoyed English so much at school I put my name down for Advanced English. The course set was Drama Throughout the Ages and I thought it would be wonderful.

What a sad, disillusioned creature I was after the first lecture. A doleful, almost moribund lady enveloped the room with her gloomy aura. More students had enrolled for her lectures than for any other, and she hoped to shake us off. She was completely lacking in animation and her voice was toneless and her eye lacklustre. She asked us to produce for the next week one of Shakespeare's plays as it might have been written by the Ancient Greeks. What a floorer! Even so, we liked English and we hung on like grim death. Only two were persuaded to slip over to French. They had a whale of a time with a mad little woman who was given to being nosy about the students' love affairs and was as much alive as the other was dead. If our lecturer had been my warden it might have been better, although her students said that her voice was so soft that it was impossible to hear unless you sat within two yards of her. Both of them were Scottish, and seemed to think it was ladylike to speak without opening their mouths. It was a common failing of all the Scotswomen on the staff excepting one. She was our Method lecturer, Och Aye, and she had a horsey face, a very lively eye, a most compelling personality and an odd speech impediment which made it sound as if she were scrunching a particularly toothsome buttered brazil. One simply had to listen. She had a way of mesmerising the children as soon as she walked into a classroom. It looked as if she had a trick up her sleeve and one had to watch out for the rabbit.

Her students adored her, and the most limited blossomed under her guidance. She would toss her white mane and laugh away their worries. Apparently her only known enemy was another very timid little Scotswoman who took Kindergarten Music, conducted the second choir of the musical society and the orchestra. Och Aye 'played' the double bass – that is, she enjoyed herself hugely thumping out rude noises at the wrong time. She always turned up late for rehearsals and scratched about like an old hen before she was ready. As one of the most senior and valued members of the staff it ill-became anyone to tick her off, but I'm told the atmosphere was very strained at times. I was never there, but on the few occasions when I saw and heard the orchestra in action it was easy to believe. Och Aye's abandon was pre-eminent. She was the only Scotswoman who boasted no doctorate. The others seemed to have lost all their joy and zest for life in acquiring theirs.

The English ladies on the staff were much more alive. One of the oldest took Hygiene. She recommended massaging castor oil into the roots of the hair and had a wonderful head of black hair to prove the benefit thereof. She was rising sixty and proud of it. 'When you're feeling cheap and the children seem like a seething mass of little monsters take a box of chocolates and a juicy novel and go to bed,' was another of her maxims.

The Biology lecturer was a hilarious little bod who hopped around squeaking, 'Train the mind, don't fill it!' If she turned up late for a lecture and we were hanging about gossiping she would rampage round the lab shouting, 'Why aren't you using your eyes and learning all you can instead of wasting your time?' Her lectures were great fun and she was known to be a great wit and leg puller in private.

Attached to the College was also Auntie Kitty. The names of students with outstanding accents or speech defects were reported to her, and so, in addition to the odd lecture on Speech Training she winkled out the students she wanted for private tuition. The people so honoured were ragged to death by the others, needless to say.

Author with friend Mac.

It was decided that there should be a verse-speaking competition, but with volunteers, as entrants were thin on the ground. I loved poetry and had a good memory and was eventually prodded into enrolling. Whilst waiting my turn for the preliminary heat I peered through the doorway and saw the 'judges'. It struck me as hilariously funny to see the lecturers who were notorious as mumblers sitting there with Squeaker in solemn judgement. The student who was in just before me had forgotten her words, and I was called in before I'd straightened my face. I stood there and looked them in the eye, doing my utmost to remember that it was really an awe-inspiring occasion. It was useless. After the first few lines I was choked with laughing and had to make my excuses and retreat. A great pity, as I knew every word and liked the pieces chosen, and the girl who came top eventually was not sure of the words. She was resident in another hostel and was surprised not to have me competing in the finals, as we'd both been well-received as elocutionists on previous occasions. I explained that my sense of humour had let me down.

By the end of the first year my friend Mac and I were down to our last twopence. There seemed to be innumerable subscriptions demanded towards presents for all and sundry. We'd bought our train tickets, to be sure of them, and I'd sent an S.O.S. home explaining the situation, but the letter containing financial relief didn't arrive until the late evening post on the night before we broke up. There were midnight feasts being held all over the place, but apart from a bag of cherries we'd nothing between us to contribute, and we didn't like to be out-and-out scroungers.

However, no students were in their rooms by midnight, and Mac and I decided to make apple-pie beds for them to come back to. At the end of the corridor we found masses of junk thrown out by students who were leaving, old tins, stockings, jars of make-up half-used and so on. We had plenty of scope, and we went to work with a will. Stockings tied to chair legs and beds made booby traps, tins under the bottom sheets or left where stealthy feet sent them flying to the accompaniment of startled screams all had the desired effect. We removed the bulb from the light in the loo (the only place where lights were permitted after 10.30 p.m.) and smeared turtle oil cream on the seat. We sprinkled sand on top of that and decided that would do. Armed with torches, innocent smiles and our cherries we padded round all the hostel and looked in at the various 'midnights' offering our cherries now and again. By this guile we managed to establish our innocence and then we went back to our cubicles to wait for the others to come up to bed. Startled cries and screams came like music to our ears and Mel's cry, after trying the light switch three times, was a distracted, 'Stella, Stella, somebody's been sick in the George!'

I'm sure we were less sophisticated at nineteen than many girls of thirteen are these days. Mac's cubicle was on one side of mine and Aileen's on the other. Aileen always had some chocolate about and Mac would scratch her toe nail on the cubicle wall and wait for Aileen to whisper, 'What's that? Can you hear it?'

'No,' Mac would answer. 'Go to sleep.'

'Listen, it's there again. It sounds like a mouse.'

'Well, what do you expect with all that chocolate about?' At which Aileen was scared stiff.

The two of them were poles apart, one a very forthright Lancashire girl, the other an over-protected only child from North London. It was very hard to keep the peace. Aileen was always nattery to be off in good time, Mac delighted in last-minuting. Aileen loved a fug and never made her bed properly, Mac stripped hers to the mattress and opened her window so wide that things blew all over the place. If we went to town together Mac would stand for ages looking at the model gown of her choice, and subsequently send a diagram and detailed description of it home. Her mother would buy some beautiful material in Blackburn market and copy the dress for a few shillings. Aileen could 'do' a shop window in one sweeping glance and then would suggest taking the tube. Mac liked walking – at her own pace.

Aileen, as a Londoner was able to go home for the day at weekends and we were often invited to go with her. Her parents were extremely kind and generous, and it was a very pleasant change from hostel life. We fed on the fat of the land, and brought back homemade Cornish pasties to eat when we got back to College.

We were allowed odd weekends off if we had written permission from our parents, and I went on these occasions to stay with the family whose name my aunt had given me. There I met the tall, thin, agonizingly shy young man who was eventually to become my spouse. But our relationship began with mutual loathing of each other's names, and disbelief, almost, of each others' temperaments. We could not have been more unlike, but he had a little mongrel bitch, and my fondness for animals made a bond which gradually blossomed into more, I think to our mutual astonishment.

Teaching practice was a great eye-opener. I had seen a good deal of teaching before I was made aware that free discipline was the modern trend. My experience at home had all been in the school I'd attended myself. The building was quite attractive, the rooms light and airy. Big yards, covered play shelters for wet days and little gardens for each class made it a very pleasant setting. The atmosphere inside was of happy industry and the staff worked to a system understood and appreciated by all. The teachers were fond of the tiny headmistress, and had her backing and encouragement. The whole scheme of work was logical and the children progressed happily through the school, knowing just where they were. By the time they left, all but the subnormal had reached a good standard of reading, writing and arithmetic, enjoyed singing and games and had progressed through the recognised stages to a high degree of physical education.

Compared with these days the handwork was more stereotyped and limited, but the girls had learnt to knit and sew and the boys to use a ruler and make simple boxes.

Odd children who were persistently awkward were usually licked into shape by the second year, and 'up the stairs to the headmistress' usually meant slapped legs if nothing more. The very thought was often a deterrent.

I was therefore astonished when faced with a class of five-year-olds in London who were used to playing their teacher up all the time. She was twenty-five, a veteran to me, and explained that it was a free discipline school and the charming woman who was the head seemed to like it if no one else did. I certainly didn't. It was horse work, and there seemed to be a complete lack of cohesion in the school.

In order to save money on fares we walked miles each day to our schools and then chose the least expensive places for midday meals. We were allowed one and sixpence each day, but at a certain Tom Thompson's we could sit amongst the bus drivers and eat a filling meal for a shilling. The money we saved was spent in an orgy at the sales. It would have been better spent on bus fares, for we were absolutely worn out by the time we'd finished school practice.

In our second year the students from my old hostel were split up amongst the others, as Brontë Hall was to be enlarged, and all the cubicles made into study bedrooms with wash basins. I had been appointed deputy senior student of Brontë and as such was in charge of the Brontë students now living in Somerville. The senior student was in the habit of taking to her bed when any extra job cropped up, so I found myself carrying a good deal more responsibility than I'd expected.

It was Brontë's turn to put on the College play, and with the students in several different hostels this became an additional problem. I was very keen to put the play on, as I thought it would be a good way of keeping the Brontë students united, but it meant borrowing someone else's common room for meetings and eventual rehearsals, and no one was keen on that.

Our old warden, now out of residence, suggested letting our turn slip by, but I was very reluctant. She asked me if I would go with her to an interview with the Principal, and whilst we were waiting together outside Miss Hawtrey's room I realized just how nervous she was. I was remembering my interview with Miss Hawtrey when I applied for Avery Hill, and her remarks that I might get a chance to work on the College play. I'd no intention of losing the chance, although I knew that there were many difficulties. I doubt very much whether she remembered me, but as Sir Charles Hawtrey's sister she must have known that the acting bug was very resilient. She was amused at my tenacity and finished the interview by saying that it was perhaps a good idea to go ahead, and that I was to ask her if we needed any help over props and so on. My old warden was greatly relieved when we emerged, shook my hand warmly and called me a brick. She had obviously been very jumpy about the interview. The Principal was known to be difficult at times and many people were scared of her. She had been an outstanding figure and done a great deal for underprivileged children for many years, and the good name of the College owed a great deal to her, but she was very weary by that time.

The choice of play was the next hurdle. It had to be a costume play because we had no men. It was the end of term before we had agreed on Clifford Bax's *The Immortal Lady*, which I felt would have an appeal for the whole College, and I knew there were students capable of taking the key roles very well.

Denys nobly typed out all the parts during the Christmas holidays. It was not to be a public performance, so we were not involved with royalties and so on.

The next term we got down to rehearsals and I knew every word in the play after a few weeks. Not so the main characters! Final school practice was on us before we'd reached anything like the standard I desired, and it was obvious that the play would not be ready for performance before Easter. Mac had agreed to make the scenery, another close friend an excellent seamstress, the costumes. We went through the wardrobe cupboard for anything that could be used, but had to buy curtain brocades for several of the 'men's' costumes. I eyed the cinema attendants critically and decided that their uniforms could be adapted for liveries in the scene at the Embassy. After much, 'Go on-you dare' on the part of Aileen and Mac I asked if I might see the manager of the cinema, and finished up with two old jackets and trousers. We turned the sleeves up and made the trousers into knee breeches. They looked fine. Wigs weren't so easy, and our efforts with cotton wool didn't bear close inspection, but the enormous hall we gave the play in was a help, as distance lent a charm. For the scene at the Venetian Embassy we drew the back cloths of the stage aside to reveal the huge marble pillars there. It looked very impressive.

Mac's efforts were lagging behind schedule. I daren't put it on later than May, as our final exams, were imminent, but my anxiety to have everyone word perfect and the set complete didn't seem to be catching. The paint was still wet on the afternoon before we put it on in the evening. Words were still being muttered frantically and last adjustments to costumes made when I was given the news that one of the students would not be able to take her part. I had to do it, as I knew the words. It was not a big part, fortunately. To my great chagrin one of my best actresses had had to give her part over to a much less talented girl because the English lecturer had intervened and complained that her work was not good enough for her to spare the time. It was the same *bête noire* who had tried to shake us off at the beginning of our course. Although she was aware enough to oblige Twink to give up her part she had shown no interest at all in the production apart from that. I was furious.

So much time spent, so many sleepless nights with words constantly racing through my brain, trips to beg and borrow here and there – even furniture from Miss Hawtrey's domain – and all for one performance, to which the public were not invited. It sounds so silly now, and yet to me it mattered more than anything else in the world.

The performance went off beautifully in the end and Miss Hawtrey sought me out afterwards to congratulate me. She said she had sat next to the author at dinner once, and if she did so again she would tell him she had seen his play produced excellently. It was all I needed for my cup to overflow. Miss Hawtrey would not have said that if she didn't mean it.

However, the strain had taken it out of me. That on top of my duties as deputy senior student had entailed endless running up and down long flights of stairs, and my heart was playing up. I was getting a lot of pain in my chest and a medical check-up resulted in my being taken off all games and P.T. for the rest of the term.

It might not have mattered to someone less active. I knew dicky hearts were in the family and had always found excessive exercise very exhausting. I went very blue in cold weather and could swim only very short distances. My doctor at home confirmed that I'd a leaky valve in my heart and ought to avoid the 'flu and rest completely when I knew I was overtired. Easier to say than to do!

By this time my relationship with H.E.M. had blossomed and he was now a qualified doctor. A much quieter type than myself, he wished earnestly that he could have borne that burden for me. I felt that my future was very uncertain. Teaching young children requires plenty of stamina and I liked to be able to take part in all their activities. I tried to lie low in the holidays, and by the end the symptoms were fading. I'm still batting thirty-five years later and have survived many attacks of the dreaded 'flu, although I can't

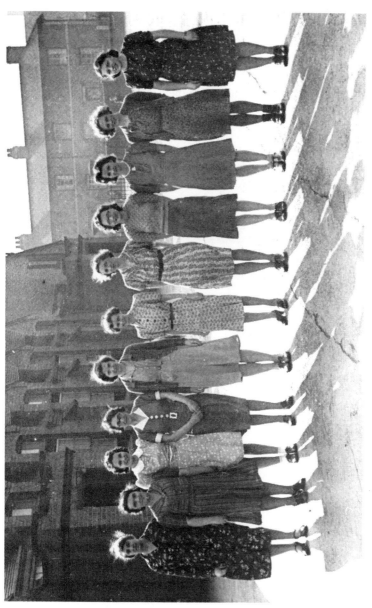

As war broke out I went back amongst my old friends at the school where I had been a Young Person in Training. (Author – second from right).

pretend not to have had some scaring bouts of pain from time to time.

We finished our College days in fine style. After the last big dance we trailed in a line across the park back to the hostel, chanting the Brontë war cry. None of the other hostels had a war cry. I said goodbye to my beloved trees in the park, in particular the aromatic poplar and the deciduous cypress. We looked our last at the old millionaire's mansion which formed the main building at College, and we saw old friends and sparring partners disperse to every part of the country.

The international scene was getting desperate and within two years the college had evacuated to Huddersfield. The enormous ballroom with the minstrels' gallery, where I had produced the play, was rendered dangerous by a bomb which had destroyed the tower at the other end of the main building. The beautiful winter gardens were left to care for themselves. It was never again to be such a lovely place as we had known when we had soaked our cane for handwork in the suite of marble mosaic rooms incorporating the Turkish bath.

I went back just after the war and saw Nissen huts between our beautiful hostels, and the destruction of the main building. I left it very sick at heart, and have not visited there since.

CHAPTER SIX

FIRST JOB

Teaching jobs were scarce at that time. We were expected to work for the local committee if posts were available, but when we were sent the list there were very few. I had applied for a job in Nottingham, and been accepted. It meant finding digs, but that would not be too difficult. Having spread my wings I didn't really want to live at home again.

Denys had offered to take me on a short cruise to Norway, and I was excited at the thought of going abroad for the first time. Within a few days of our departure I had a letter from the County Education Officer asking me to call, as there were two jobs going in local mining villages. He said that Nottingham City would understand if I sent back word, and asked me to meet the manager of one of the mines for an interview. I was very put out, and explained that our cruise was fixed for the time when he had arranged the interview. I didn't want the job, but I daren't make that too apparent, as he had a stranglehold on all the local teachers, and his reputation was not of the best.

In the end I met the colliery manager, who made snide remarks about young teachers who could afford to travel abroad when jobs were at stake. Fortunately the Education Officer told him that I had a job fixed up in Nottingham and he became a little more pleasant. But he probed into my private life and asked if I had plans for an early marriage. I wanted to bonk him on the head, but answered that I was not engaged. Knowing that my mother wanted me back home I did not like to refuse to take the job, and so a few weeks later I found myself teaching the colliery manager's very intelligent child, and meeting his charming wife.

The school year began in an atmosphere of impending doom, with the ghastly business of war ever closer, Munich and so on. Married women

57

teachers were still almost unknown in our county unless their husbands were handicapped. At the school I'd trained in there were the inevitable end-of-term strains, but by and large the spinsters there were spinsters gay. Not so at the school where I began my first real teaching. The head had intolerable problems in her home background which made her a bundle of nerves and anxiety, and this reflected on the whole staff. All their spare time seemed to be spent in grousing and criticising her, although superficially they were on good terms and the school ran like clockwork.

The children were extremely mixed. The hierarchy were those of the colliery officials and the shopkeepers. The others were all miners' children – some well-cared for, and others obviously underfed and very dirty. Even so, one of the least well-cared for had a reading age of nine when he was under six, and he made a marvellous pot at writing stories. I was told that most of his big family were T.B. He was really a delightful child to teach. On the other hand there was the little girl who came proudly in a new frock and wore nothing else until it had gone through the stages of grubby, dirty, filthy and buttonless and finally presumably, was thrown away. On the coldest days her coat was fastened with one enormous safety pin, and she arrived crying with cold, unable to cope with the pin when the others were unbuttoning their coats. Once thawed out she was very cheerful, but 'thick' in the extreme.

At Christmas we put on a concert. As most of them had recently seen Walt Disney's *Snow White* my class elected to act it. We made up the script as we went along, and we had an excellent little narrator, whose only failing was to sprinkle 'h's liberally where they were least desirable. The dwarfs each chose their own character, based on the film, and their efforts were greatly appreciated. We had a great deal of fun making costumes and a few props, and the staff and parents showed some surprise at the polished performance. To my critical eye the efforts of the older children seemed very limited and stilted in comparison, but the rest of the staff had been under the crabbing and confining influence of the head for several years. I remembered Och Aye's influence and tried to draw everything out of the children.

The following term the inspectors came and were as critical of the rigid discipline as I was myself. Trends were changing and although I deplored the chaos in the free discipline school I'd worked in in London I was sure there was room for more fun and self-expression than was encouraged in my first real job. I looked at the tetchy thirty-year-olds on the staff and dreaded that I should be squeezed into the mould. My class were reading well and doing famously with their 'sums', but at five I didn't think neatness was more important than zest for getting on. It made me furious when a child got a star for a neat book with several sums wrong and my grubby little Charles had no praise for doing twice as many sums and getting them right. If my ducks and ducklings on the frieze swam somewhat drunkenly amongst the reeds I didn't mind. The children had had a whale of a time putting them there. Och Aye had insisted that that was more value than the hectographed carefully filled-in efforts so often stuck on by the teacher in order that the room was as 'twee' and pretty as a spinster's boudoir. My head did not agree. We were poles apart.

Things at home were not too good. It was obvious that my mother's health was declining. From a buxom fifty-year-old she seemed to be shrinking. The pain in her back, which she had had from time to time, and had always associated with an accident when she was a young woman, now never left her. I tried to persuade her to see the doctor, but she seemed to be afraid. A very virulent bug hit me and knocked me for six. When the doctor called I turned to my mother and said, 'And now tell him about yourself.' He was obviously too busy to stop and examine her then, but she did promise to go to the surgery for a thorough examination. Tom's wife agreed to go with her, and she had a grave face when, later, she returned with mother from a visit to see the specialist.

It was cancer of the bowel, and an operation, whilst relieving the pain, could not save her life. Mother had not been told, but I'm sure she had guessed from the beginning of the more sinister symptoms, which had made her dread going to see the doctor.

When my sister-in-law told me I was stunned. After a very hard life mother had just reached the stage when she could take things more easily, and now she could not be expected to live more than two years at the outside, perhaps not much longer than six months. On enquiring what the operation would entail she refused to have it. At that time a colostomy was greatly dreaded. I would not have told her, as I knew that she would be spared some pain and even worse, but she was told by someone else.

It was obvious that I must plan to give more and more time to caring for her.

On the bus one day I met a staff member of my old school, where I had trained and been so happy. 'Do you know anyone who wants a job in our school?' she asked.

'Indeed, yes. I do,' was my reply.

A few days later I met tiny Miss T., the head of the old school.

'I hear you would like to come back to us, Nancy,' she said. 'There's nothing I would like more than to have you, but it is only fair to warn you that the class will be extremely difficult. They are the worst lot of children we've ever had, and no one will offer to take them on. I'm afraid the new teacher will have to face them.'

I told her of the situation at home and that it would be a help to me to be able to get home at lunch time, which was quite out of the question at the school in the mining village.

The head where I was teaching was very annoyed and took it as an insult that I wanted to move after only one year with her. In the end I told her my need to be nearer home and she accepted the fact with an ill grace.

War broke out and the town was flooded with evacuees just as term was about to start. All the local teachers were called on to help cope with the children. When I went home at teatime after a gruelling session in the town I found Mother had taken in two little Nottingham girls. She was having an awful job to keep going at all, and I was very annoyed that she should have been pushed to accept them, but I knew quite well that she was incapable of sending any child away from her door.

The two girls were bosom friends. Irene was an undersized chirpy, dirty little thing. She was scratching her head all the time and, I learned later, had escaped from the room where the infested children had been put at the evacuee centre. She was to have been placed with a younger brother and sister, but was determined to be with her Hilda, and not be looking after the little ones. I knew nothing of that. It was of paramount importance to get her cleaned up, and I got on with the job. A large sheet of newspaper spread over the table, I combed out the running lice and she caught them and squashed them. After a time she asked, 'Can I rest my head a bit? It's good fun though in'it, Aunt Nancy?' With special soap and small-toothed comb I gradually cleaned her up. Her belongings were mainly a gas mask and the poor clothes she stood up in.

Hilda was a bigger, better-nourished child, but with a much more serious disposition. She had a case, with carefully-tended clothes, and some money given by her big sister, who was her guardian. I rigged up Irene with clothes, and Mother kept pushing food down to try and fatten her up. She called Mother, 'G'anma,' and relished every morsel.

It was soon obvious that they were too much. They explored nearby building sites and came back up to the ankles in lime. They lit the emergency candle and tried to read under the bedclothes during a black-out, with the inevitable result. In the end a neighbour said she'd have the quiet one, as she had always wanted a little girl and had a bedroom to spare. Hilda went very reluctantly to a prettier room than she'd ever seen, but in spite of all her kindness the neighbour was deserted after a few days. Hilda vanished! Great alarm and despondency followed and the kind neighbour admitted that Hilda had been very frightened at the idea of sleeping alone. She had been weeping at bed time and it was obvious that separating her from her chirpy, mischievous pal had been a big mistake. She said she was worrying about her big sister at home.

An hour or so after the first alarm at her not returning from school, the police arrived. She had asked for some of her spending money to buy a pencil box, but had in fact taken a bus back to Nottingham. When her sister came in from work she found her waiting on the doorstep, and made all speed to contact the police and ask their help in letting us know what had happened. Their mother had committed suicide and two brothers were in a sanatorium. Hilda was worried in case her big sister was lonely without her, and would put her head in the gas oven as her mother had. It was a pitiful tale. As soon as she was free the sisters came together to fetch Hilda's things, and to thank us for what we had done. 'I'm sorry she didn't stay. She'd have learned a better way of life here. But I did miss her, and though

I wouldn't have done what my mother did we'd better stick together now.' We admired her very much. She was still under twenty and was carrying a great burden of responsibility.

Irene found life with us dull after Hilda's departure. 'We didn't find *her* dull. She'd a great sense of humour and trotted out priceless pearls of Nottingham dialect – 'You'll make some more soup, notcha G'anma?' and so on. A misspelt note from her mother announced the arrival of yet another baby in the family. That was it. Irene had to go and inspect her new sister. Hundreds of children had already drifted back home and she begged to join them.

We parted good friends, and she went home with rosier and fuller cheeks than she came with, and a modest collection of clean clothes. We missed her constant cheerful chatter, but it was a relief, in view of mother's worsening condition.

Although she liked to get up before midday and to make a meal for when I came in from school, all the rest of the work was done by a kindly Mrs Evans. Soon Mother's attempts to keep going were frustrated by her constant pain. When the air raid siren went I helped her downstairs and into our makeshift shelter in the cellar. Even with an old rug down and a cushioned cane chair the deadly chill soon reached one's bones. Denys had joined the R.A.F. and I was alone with Mother at night. After a few wretched trails into the cellar it was obvious that Mother was not fit to leave her bed. It was not our little town the droning monsters were after. I put out all the lights and sat by her bedside. 'My life is over,' she said. 'You go down into the cellar, your life is before you.' It was the first time she had admitted that she knew that her number was up. I pretended not to notice. 'I'm sure we're safe enough here,' I answered, and she found some joke to pass over the dismal revelation.

H.E.M. was qualified and doing a houseman's job at Folkstone when we became engaged. I told Mother, and her comment was, 'I'm glad you've got engaged. He'll make you a good side.' How right she was! His temperament was the complete reverse of her own, but she was an excellent judge of character. My brothers all got on well with him, but he seized up with strangers and cast an icy silence on some friends I tried to link up with

The author and H. – Christmas 1941.

him. My sister, a great prophetess of gloom, knew more of his background and family than the rest of my family. She was certain a marriage between us would never work out, and tried to talk me out of it. With a war just begun the whole future was uncertain and we made no plans for an early marriage.

I wore no ring at first, and when I did, my old friends on the staff at school were staggered. I'd never mentioned his name, and they thought my life was completely wrapped up in school, my mother's illness and W.V.S. and Toc H wartime services.

Indeed my life was hectic enough. Along with a group of young women I'd been asked to form a Toc H League of Women Helpers branch in the town. The local hospital was bulging with soldiers, and we ran a twice-weekly library service there. We also ran a canteen in a huge, almost derelict house near the cricket field in the centre of the town. As the first Job Master I was not only involved in doing the jobs, but also in organizing rotas and arranging visitors for lonely old people and so on. I was roped in to do a weekly stint at the central Report Centre. This was in the cellar of another large house, and one was deadly cold by the end of the session. The phone rarely went excepting for practice 'alerts', when it was necessary to ring up a particular A.R.P. post and tell them all to be ready to cope with imaginary incendiaries etc.

Two or three of the Toc. H. League of Women Helpers (always known as L.W.H.) got themselves engaged to the lads they chatted to over library books in hospital or baked beans on toast at the canteen. The local Toc H. male members decided the initials stood for Ladies Wanting Husbands.

We enjoyed the work, but it was exhausting in the extreme, and always begun after a full working day. Mrs Foster or one of my sisters-in-law used to sit with Mother whilst I did these various jobs.

As Miss T. had warned me, the class I faced now contained a group of real tinkers. It must have been a case of 'birds of a feather', for they all lived in the same street and must have polished up their villainy on the neighbours when they weren't plaguing me.

Their ring-leader was an outsize pudding-faced boy, whose every gesture was taken in by his cronies. Amongst them was one Jackie McAdam whose name has haunted me down the years. He was so devilishly funny, as well as being just devilish. Physically he was the same type as Irene, the evacuee, but in addition to his thin, quicksilver little body he had the boldest blue eyes, almost capable of convincing even me of his innocence at times, and a comical squirt of hair which rose in painful surprise that anyone could associate iniquity with its owner.

I was warned at the outset that 'That Jackie McAdam would take some watching.' Indeed he did, for he never seemed to be in the same place for two minutes, and where Jackie went disaster followed. It was said that the gang were the children of jail birds and their mothers were no better than they should have been. Pudding Face was just a born rebel, and had the art of non co-operation off to a turn, and what he did or didn't do the rest copied. They'd got away with it for three years and didn't intend changing the system for my benefit. They were virtually all at the same attainment level – practically zero – and I had them lumped together in one group to start with.

One ill-starred day they had been particularly noxious, and I was at the end of my tether. I threatened that if I had any more trouble from the group I'd trounce the lot of them. To my dismay I was soon in the position of having them in a row with their tough little backsides waiting for my weary hand to carry out the threat. It was very much more painful to me than to them. One miserable little ferret of a lad had done no more than giggle at Pudding Face's insolence, but I had to give him a token pat on his rear, as he was in the same group. He gave me a very dirty look and made out that he was deeply offended.

On the way home the next day I was obliged to dismount my bicycle by a puny ten-year-old who deliberately cycled across my path. He shook his fist at me and said very menacingly, 'Eh, Ilett, thee leave my kid broother alooan!'

It was only the beginning. After that he turned up regularly, shook his fist at me and then departed. It was not only on my return from school. He seemed to have an uncanny foreknowledge of my movements, and to appear unexpectedly, shake his fist and depart. I didn't like it, but it was obvious that kid brother felt protected by the challenging look on his face. At a Toc.

Mother relaxing – first left.

H.L.W.H. meeting I told them of my undesirable 'follower'. The young padré thought it was hugely funny and roared with laughter at my discomfiture. 'All well and good for you to laugh,' I said, 'but I'm beginning to have nightmares with that little threatening figure in them, though I must admit he grins as often as not now. How can I stop it?'

The padré thought for a moment. 'Well, I'd give a courtly little bow and say, "Goodday, my little man."' It worked. The next meeting was the last. He was taken completely by surprise and left me in peace afterwards.

About this time I bumped into Bunty, an old school friend. She was tiny, but was teaching senior boys in a very tough mining village. I wondered how she coped with big lads when I was finding eight to nine-year-olds such hard going. 'Oh, I don't wear myself out smacking their behinds,' she said, 'I keep a heavy Dunlop P.E. shoe in the cupboard. It hurts them, but doesn't hurt me. I just reach for it and they shut up.'

I thanked her for the tip, but was a bit doubtful about taking the same line. However, I wrapped one up in a duster and hid it in the cupboard. The next time I was really exasperated I used it on Pudding Face's nether end. He was most impressed, and so were his gang. Bunty was right, it didn't have to come out often. Pudding Face's work improved. I complimented him and said it would be nice when everybody tried as hard. It was sweet music to his ears, and his behaviour became positively exemplary. I said I hoped all his group would copy his good behaviour, and he began to tick off those who were still troublesome.

It was unbelievable, but all the staff noticed the change, and I confided in them about Bunty's advice and the P.E. shoe. 'I don't think Miss T. would approve, but it is worth its weight in gold.'

McAdam was the only outstanding rebel after that, and he was quite incorrigible. He was licking his nails and rubbing red chalk in one day, instead of writing. I ticked him off and he said, 'Well, women does it.' I sent him out to wash, and he stayed in the corridor doing a clog dance. The head heard him and fetched him up to her room. To my astonishment a messenger came a few minutes later to ask if Miss T. might borrow my P.E. shoe. I'd no idea that she knew of its existence. But Jackie did another little dance outside the door before coming in again. He was quite unabashed.

'She 'it me burritdidn'urt.'

He later confided, 'Ah wis' Ah were a woman.'

I was most intrigued. 'Why on earth would you want to be a woman, Jackie?' I asked.

'So's Ah could 'ave a babby.'

'But what would you do with a baby, Jackie?'

'Ah s'ould gi'e it soom milk, like me Anty Iris does,' he said, rolling his blue eyes soulfully at the thought of suckling an infant.

I was about pickled with subdued laughter at the thought, but a virtuous little Shirley Temple of a girl shot out, 'Miss Ilett, he's not fit to have a baby at all. He's not fit to be a daddy. He'd never go out and work for his family. He never does his work at school.'

'Miss, Ah should work if Ah 'ad a babby. Ah can work if Ah wants to,' he assured me very earnestly.

It was my chance, 'Then prove it to us, Jackie. Just sit there and really work and show us.'

He grabbed his pencil, stuck out his tongue and did an astonishingly good writing exercise. But he was only proving that he could. His halo soon slipped.

When an inspector came they were all on their best behaviour, and he obviously thought they were a grand set of kids. 'I like coming here,' he said. 'Why do you think I like this class?'

Jackie's hand shot up and he answered, ''Cos we're 'appy.'

'Yes, indeed,' said the inspector. I thought of our forays and laughed.

Miss T. thanked me on the quiet for the loan of the P.E. shoe. She didn't like using a cane, and her frail little hand suffered even more than mine when trying to leave a salutory impression on the seats of the black sheep. We had a good laugh over Jackie's agreement with the inspector.

At home the situation was grimmer than ever. Little Mrs Evans, who was devoted to my mother, burst into tears one day and told me she would have to stop coming. She said she could not face watching her die. Mother was in bed all the time now. My two sisters-in-law who lived near came in once a day to help with the nursing, but I couldn't leave the house unattended for hours a day, and I couldn't give up my job. As Mother woke several times each night I was in and out of her bedroom to give her a drink or change dressings every two or three hours. Although she rarely called, I was a very light sleeper, and always knew when she was in distress.

When the situation seemed at its blackest Tom came in with the news that he'd found a reliable teenage girl who was willing to come and live in. When the thin, long-faced Jane arrived I found it hard to believe she was only nineteen. She had a front tooth missing and looked dragged down, and twice her age.

By the end of a week she looked immeasurably better, and she smiled and chatted away. When it was her time off she visited her family, but said she preferred to be with us. Their diet at home was mainly 'tatties', she said, and she shared a room with two rough younger sisters. She took to Mother, and faced all there was to face, learning how to cook from my instructions at breakfast time and keeping the house clean and tidy.

At supper time one night she said, 'There's something I must tell you, Miss Nancy, only you're so good I don't know what you'll think of me.' I assured her that I was not good and in any case was in no position to sit in

One of my last pictures of Mother.

judgment on anyone. As far as I was concerned she had come when I was in great need and proved to be a very reliable help.

'Well, I thought you might guess when our Mary came last week,' she continued. 'Didn't you notice what she called me?' Mary was a fair little two-year-old Jane had called her little sister when she brought her to see me on her day off. I rattled my brains and remembered the child had called Jane 'Mummy,' but I'd thought nothing of it at the time. The other members of Jane's family were boisterous and very dark. Jane was mousy and quite unlike any of the rest of the slap-happy brood.

She spent the next hour telling me all about herself.

'The others are not really my brothers and sisters. I can't stand them. I like to read and be quiet, but there's never a chance at home. My Mum fell in love with a young minister and he loved her and wanted to marry her. My Grandma didn't like his religion and wouldn't agree to a wedding. Mum got pregnant, but they still couldn't marry, and I was a love-child. A year or two later my Mum met Dad and he said he'd marry her and take me for his own, if they moved away from the district.

'But he never really loved me. When the others came along they were tough and noisy and I was pushed on one side. As soon as I left school I found a job in service and I left home and lived in at a big country house. We had a lot of fun in the servants' quarters and we saw a lot going on when they had house parties. I'd plenty to eat and didn't have to work too hard. I lived with my Grandma when I wasn't at work, but when I'd my time off in the afternoon I went for walks over the hills. I met a young shepherd called Duncan, and I used to meet him as often as I could. He was very kind and gentle and we fell in love. Honest, I didn't know what we did was wrong, Miss Nancy. He said we did it because we loved each other. When I missed, I didn't know why. It's hard to believe, but nobody had told me.

'We were making beds one day – another maid and me – and under a mattress we found a little book all about having a baby. I read it through and knew that I must be having one, and when I told Duncan he said he'd marry me and was sure his boss would let us have a cottage. But I was only sixteen, and when I told me Grandma she flew in a terrible temper. She told me then how I came to be born. She said Duncan must be a wicked man to get me with a baby when I was only sixteen. But Duncan wasn't wicked. He was only seventeen, but he worked hard and his boss said he'd help us to get a few things together and there was a tiny cottage we could have. It were no use. Mam didn't remember how she'd had me. She backed up Grandma and said I'd not to see Duncan again. He was crying when we said goodbye.

'I was seventeen when Mary was born. I had her at my Grandma's, and old doctor came. It was terrible, and I screamed out for me Mam, but old doctor said, "You wasn't crying out for your Mam when you got yourself pregnant." But our Mary were a pretty little babby and me Mam said we'd move south and she'd pretend she was Mary's Mam so I could get a job!

'Mary calls our Mam, "Mam" like everybody else, but she calls me "Mummy" so people's bound to know. I had to tell you, Miss Nancy. I thought you must know by now!'

Poor Jane! No wonder she had looked such a sorry sight when she came. Now she was feeding properly and could give most of her modest wage to her family to pay for Mary's keep, the situation at her home improved. I gave her some more attractive clothes and she began to blossom. Mary was an intelligent little thing and on Jane's half-day often came to see me with her Mummy. On one occasion Jane's large, exuberantly-proportioned Mam came to thank me for helping Jane. She brought two of her sloe-eyed strapping daughters to meet me. I can well believe that the tiny house they lived in was full to overflowing, both physically and psychologically, and could understand why Jane cut short her time off and came back to read in our quieter house.

A great deal had changed since the days when all the family were at home and the strains of the 'band' attracted many of the neighbours to swell our ranks. More often than not when I was at home I sat weaving on a free heddle with one ear cocked in case Mother made any sounds of distress. As the long winter dragged to its end her attempts to eat were always followed by vomiting and her body continued to waste away. Her features became very fine-drawn under the yellowing skin, and she looked at her hands and joked that at long last they were without work stains – the hands of a lady. When old friends came to visit her they gasped at the change in her as they entered the bedroom. She was a great actress and always put on a brave front. They invariably came out smiling at some parting shot she threw at them. She was utterly spent after these attempts at bravado, but was quite determined to play the game and pretend she didn't know.

Dear Aunty Fran came from the south a few weeks before the end. She was shaken to the core, and grasped my hand to keep her pecker up when in the bedroom. 'None of us knows what we shall come to,' she said afterwards with her eyes full of tears. 'What a life she's led, and how courageous she has always been. To think she can talk to me of plans for a holiday together next year! She's trying to keep my spirits up.'

Uncle Harry, Mother's eldest brother, had not visited us since shortly after my father's death twenty-one years earlier, but I wrote to him and he came over. In his sixties he still had an amazingly beautiful and steady tenor voice. It was natural for him to announce his presence by going up the stairs singing. Mother tried to respond with a pitiful attempt at singing – her first for over a year. I choked back my own tears as I followed Uncle up to the room, knowing that he'd have a terrible shock when he saw her. It was not so easy for him to sing as he came down again.

My two sisters-in-law kept up daily visits and the district nurse came as frequently. The doses of morphia were stepped up and it didn't seem possible for her to keep going. Tom offered to stay up at nights, but with loyal Jane I was able to cope. I knew when she was going because she grasped my hand and said, 'But it's you kids I'm bothered about. What will you do when I'm gone?' I told Tom he'd better stay that night, and at midnight I asked Jane to fetch Eric. Mother went shortly after he came. They had both been very good sons and were devoted to her.

She looked extremely beautiful in her coffin. A friend who had visited regularly with bunches of fragrant herbs brought more to put about the house.

My own relief at her release from pain was almost joy by the following morning. It was as if her old gaiety were permeating the house and telling me not to mourn. But all my defences broke down at the funeral service.

The church was packed, and Harry's voice rose above all the others as he sang to her. Doug came, and I heard him sobbing helplessly – no doubt remembering his shortcomings, as I did my own.

When everyone had gone I faced a lonely prospect. Jane would have to go, and the house would be full of memories.

I could not cope with children and keep up all my voluntary work as well as full time teaching, but there was a great shortage of accommodation in the town. In the end I arranged for a sergeant and his wife to share the house in return for some domestic help. We had fruit and vegetables from the garden, which they shared, and they settled very happily – surprised that I didn't want any money from them.

I found another job for Jane – looking after a neighbour's children, but she came to me for a testimonial a little later saying she could earn more money in a factory. The last I saw of her she was married to an overseer and pushing a smart pram with little Mary trotting beside. She looked very happy.

London was taking a terrible bashing about that time and my sergeant's wife was very anxious about her mother. She had an urge to go and try to persuade her to leave London for somewhere safer, as her health was suffering badly.

With his wife gone, the sergeant moved back to barracks and I was alone again.

CHAPTER SEVEN

THE MISSION AND MARRIAGE

Miss T. had asked me to take charge of a branch of the school which had to be opened in a mission hall a mile away on the outskirts of the town. With me was to go the uncertificated teacher who had the 'baby' class. This meant splitting the sixty children aged five to eight into two lots, with Sarina taking the younger half and me coping with the rest. Sarina's method was simple – do what you can with those who are interested and let the others do what the h--- they liked. As we were separated by only a wooden partition this meant that I had to teach above the shindy, and drag by the scruff of the neck the children who had never thought of working until I tackled them. It was not easy. The caretaker was nuts, and didn't like coping with the boiler on cold winter mornings. One of us would have to cycle a mile or more to drag him from his bed whilst the other played the piano for the children to sing, skip and dance to in an attempt to keep warm. We always tried first to coax the boiler into life ourselves, but were not often successful. It sticks in my mind that His Nibs, the caretaker, would extol the virtues of Bemax to us, and tell us how it kept him going in the winter. We used to wish he'd try something which got him up in time to do his job.

The trying conditions at school, no doubt coupled with reaction following my mother's death, and returning to an empty house at night finally took their toll. Violent pains in my back and side persuaded me to send for the doctor, and I went down with pleurisy. I went back to school before I was really fit and was on my back again within forty-eight hours.

It was obviously not a good thing to be living alone, and someone asked me if I would take in an evacuee mother and two boys. I agreed that they might come on the same terms as the sergeant and his wife.

Mrs Botcher was an amply-proportioned, rather pop-eyed blonde. Her elder boy, about ten, was a quiet, pleasant lad whom she pecked at continually. She couldn't forgive him for being a bed-wetter, and needing 'potting' at about eleven at night. He never had a minute's peace in her company, which was probably the root cause of his affliction. The younger boy was a lively four-year-old, who was completely ruined by his mother. In return she demanded constant displays of affection, and would have him sitting with his legs round her waist and his arms round her neck, 'Hold me tighter!' she would demand. 'Love me, love me, love me!'

No doubt the poor woman missed her husband. He was a very pleasant fellow who came to visit as often as he could. He was very fond of his family, but annoyed his wife very much by spending several hours of his time with a daughter who was billeted elsewhere. Mrs Botcher would grind her teeth in jealousy when she knew he was in the town but not with her. She told me how he waited on her at home and how proud he was of her.

Her idea of looking after the house consisted of reading endless books and nursing the four-year-old. She admitted she'd never had such a lazy time, nor been so well off financially. For me the situation soon palled. I got on well with the elder boy, but the young one was a little tartar, and the shrieking at one and the embarrassing scenes with the other got under my skin as much as her laziness. It reached me on the grapevine that she'd been in several homes and always driven them mad.

Shortly before Christmas Sheffield was heavily bombed twice. At the outbreak of war my mother had been approached by a relation who had in-laws in Sheffield and asked if they might come to us in case of emergency. I was told the day after the second bombing that the family concerned were homeless. One child had been killed, an older boy injured and the mother and little girl were suffering badly from shock. They wanted to come to me.

It was a terrible situation. There was not room in the house for them and the Botchers. I told Mrs Botcher and she flew into a rage. Her husband had just arranged to come over for Christmas, but when he arrived he said his family must go elsewhere under the circumstances. I was bitterly sorry for him, and just as sorry for the next woman who was landed with his spouse and their sons.

Needless to say, it was not all beer and skittles with my next houseful.

It was arranged that Don, the husband, should come over at weekends only. As the injured boy was in hospital at first I was left with the little girl and her mother, Nora. They both needed rest and care, and I did all I could to help them. Nora had been a gay spark as a young girl, but was now grieving over the loss of the younger son and the lameness of the elder one. In a short time the elder boy joined us. I was sorry for the lad. He'd lost his brother, his home and was separated from his friends. He was at a loose end and tended to wander off on his crutches and find something to throw stones at to relieve his feelings.

We got on well together until Don decided to leave the hostel in Sheffield and come and stay with us. He assumed immediately that he was head of the household. He belonged to a very close-knit group of people he referred to as the Brethren, and was sure that I was not safe until drawn into the net. He began to preach in the open in the town, and I wouldn't have minded that, but he preached hard at me, and I found his aggressive cocksureness and his blindness to Nora's condition very irksome. She had some internal injuries, which eventually killed her, but was putting a brave face on things. Her spirits had begun to rise and she was beginning to enjoy going out a bit. She had come back from the shops one day and had pushed her hat back to a jaunty angle and was recounting an amusing incident to me. We were both laughing when Don walked in. 'What's all the silly noise about?' he said. 'What is there to laugh about? Take that foolish hat off your head.'

I could have crowned him. Nora's smiles had seemed a great triumph to me.

A very garrulous relation of mine turned up out of the blue and begged a night's lodging. She talked at me until very late and we were in the room under Nora's bedroom. Had I known of her coming I would have lit a fire in the sitting room, but it was too cold to go in there. The next morning Don raged at me for making a noise when they were trying to sleep.

On another occasion a policeman called to say he could see a chink of light through the black-out curtains. He banged on the front door and Don came storming down the stairs. He was very rude to the poor copper, who was only doing his duty. I said that I was the householder and I was sorry about the light. I thanked the policeman and shut the door.

I'd had about enough of Don, and told him I was not used to insulting people who came to my home. A short time later he told me that he didn't consider they owed me any debt of gratitude. The home they'd lost was a modern one and much nicer than mine. His 'Brethren' were collecting for him and they'd have a lovely home again after the war. He said this in front of his wife, who was quite shaken by his outburst and said quietly that she was very grateful for the help I'd given her.

The winter months seemed endless and with one thing and another I was very tired. Since my mother's death I had seemed drained and unable to show enthusiasm about anything. Sarina, my colleague, kept hinting that I ought to get married and give up the old home. I'd kept it on partly in order to have a home for Doug and Denys, but full of evacuees it was not much of a home for them on the rare occasions when they came.

At Easter I was invited to spend a holiday with my fiancé at the home of his married brother. What a relief it was to get away from school, canteen and hospital jobs and my domestic troubles. I began to thaw a bit emotionally and to feel more alive again. We decided to get married in the summer holiday and collect some things of our own before the shops were completely empty of good furniture and furnishings.

Sarina was thrilled. She had had a tragically abortive affair when quite young, and was now tied to an ailing mother, an irascible father, and a half-witted brother, born when her mother had a nervous breakdown. She was determined to have as much excitement as possible out of my wedding. 'You'll wear white?' she asked. I said it was not likely. I'd have everything to see to and the quieter things were the better.

That didn't suit at all. 'Oh, your mother would have wanted you in white. Althea will expect to be a bridesmaid and one of your cousins. I'll help.' I still was not keen, but she browbeat me unmercifully. 'Tom can give you away. Your brothers can be ushers. Everybody will expect you to have a nice wedding. Your husband will be in uniform. It will be lovely.'

In the end I complied. With one brunette and one auburn bridesmaid I decided on gold taffeta with a tiny sprig of flowers for Althea and Cousin

Kay's dresses. I bought the material in Nottingham and got a Harris tweed suit to wear on our honeymoon at the same time. Forty-eight hours later clothes were rationed. I hadn't got any material for my own dress. But Sarina had the answer. She knew someone in the trade who could let her have some silk for my dress. I couldn't stop her.

Her present to me was to make an eiderdown and bedspread to match, if I would like to get the material. We bought that – a beautiful Persian rose pattern on a dove grey and green shot silk – miles of it, it seemed to me, in the nick of time as far as coupons were concerned.

For some time after, Sarina cycled up to school with her cycle basket piled high with whatever thing she was making for me, and her shrimp-girl hat only just visible over the top. She was in her element. Her charges got noisier and noisier, and I was scared stiff Miss T. would pay us a visit and find Sarina happily sewing whilst the kids played *Hamlet*. She was always 'just getting something ready for the machine.'

After the bedspread and eiderdown she made a beautiful nightdress case and a cover for an old blanket chest, and used up the last scraps to make me a lavender lady for the dressing table. Actually, her own gifts included two beautiful hand-made cushions and a biscuit barrel. She was very generous, and was terribly excited all that term.

Another of her little ploys was to wheedle a few eggs out of the man who kept a poultry farm next to our mission building 'school'. It was very illicit and I was always scared stiff as I took home my share of the booty – usually three eggs.

We had had 'loo' trouble in the winter. The building was designed for use at weekends for two services and a Sunday school session. One loo outside and one inside were considered adequate. Sarina was sure we ought to have more, and began to agitate. The old doctor who came to look into the matter was not impressed by Sarina's verbosity. Their conversation was very amusing. Although I was officially in charge I refused to be drawn in.

However, there was a very long snowy spell during our second winter there, when the dear little boys filled the outside loo with snow, and blocked the whole system. It then became the popular sport to ask for a piece of toilet paper and go for a nice little trot along the road to the house of the noble Mum who had offered to help out in our emergency.

The ring leader of the 'baddies' in Sarina's class used to chalk himself, the floor, his neighbours and anything he could find. He never joined the elect round Sarina's knee, so he learned nothing. Every so often his mother complained about his going home all colours of the rainbow, but Sarina declared he was a menace and she could do nothing with him. To our great relief he caught the mumps, and comparative peace reigned. As Sarina was lining them up prior to morning school some time later she gave an ugly agonized shriek. I rushed to the door, thinking she'd been injured. 'What's wrong?' I called.

'My God! It's back!' was her retort.

The summer term flew quickly. I was sorting out and disposing of the belongings of the family in addition to trying to prepare my future home. The evacuees were to be allowed to rent the old house, as one of my married brothers had decided to buy it. They wanted their own things and I wanted to make a fresh start somewhere else. Trying to get a flat was like asking for the moon. In the end I managed to rent two rooms with the use of bathroom and kitchen. I had to cycle three miles to stain and polish the floors there, the good woman wouldn't give me a key and was out as often as not when I got there.

Clearing out at home included the melancholy business of going through all mother's songs. I couldn't face it, and asked Denys when he came home. His method was simple. He burned the lot. My father's old oak desk went to one brother, the Queen Anne table to another and so on. The poor old rose wood piano with green pleated silk behind the fancy front was really not worth keeping. A friend who had just bought an isolated cottage gave us £1 for it. She put it in a tiny room and called it her music room.

Tom knew of a shop somewhere in poor shattered Sheffield where there were still a few good pianos left. I went with a piano tuner to choose one for our new home, and have always been glad that I did so.

I had bought bedding before things were so scarce, and we had gone to London to order furniture as soon as I'd succeeded in finding the rooms.

What a stupid mistake! We had heard of a well-known firm's reserve supply of good furniture and decided to buy a bedroom and dining-suite and a carpet there. It did not occur to me that the things would have to be crated and sent by rail. They arrived one very windy day and I had a message that the things were at our home waiting to be unpacked and the crates returned to the station.

I was never more thankful for having good-natured brothers. Eric brought a friend and came to my rescue, but the packing straw blew up to the roof of the house and all over the garden. The owners of the house watched with baleful eyes from the window, and Eric said, 'I give you a month at the outside with that couple.'

It was a bad beginning, but I gradually got things settled in and the two rooms looked very attractive. With the piano and an oak chest I'd bought for my future husband's microscope and so on there was not room for more than one fireside chair, but I knew I'd be alone most of the time.

Anything left in the old house was to be used by the evacuees until they'd replaced it with their new belongings.

Term ended and I'd a few days to prepare for the wedding itself. Eric had arranged for a reception. Tom was to give me away. Denys and Doug arrived, and Cousin Kay. The best man, my future brother-in-law, was to spend the night before the wedding with the bridegroom in our new home, and I'd booked for all the other 'in-laws' at a hotel in the town. A friend offered to put me up for my last night as a spinster.

Claremont was bulging, as Mrs Foster had taken under her wing a pathetic quartet of evacuees. They were two very old nurses (always dressed in pre-1914 nannies' gear) and little twin four-year-old girls.

Kay was invited to sleep there, and Althea was back there until she began her first appointment in Hereford.

Always a poor sleeper, I didn't sleep a wink the night before the wedding. I was tired to dropping point, having arranged for food for the two men at the new home and seen the in-laws settled in at the hotel. I went to Claremont to see Althea and Kay into their bridesmaids' dresses and they scuttled off with the Fosters down to Potter Street. In the end it was one of the old nurses who saw me properly veiled and into the taxi with Tom. I felt like a black-eyed Susan rather than a radiant bride.

Denys and Doug were looking self-consciously smart as they handed

The Wedding Day.

out hymn books and showed people to their places. The sun streamed down and the service passed off without any hitches. My very new husband squeezed my hand reassuringly as we walked out into the sunshine, and all my friends from church, school and Toc. H. were outside to wish us well.

Tom, normally an ace-raconteur made a very poor speech. I think he'd been awake all night worrying about it. My husband, normally agonizingly shy, replied with all the confidence in the world. In spite of wartime restrictions Eric had put on a marvellous meal, and the two families, so totally different, seemed to get on very well with each other.

It was a very early wedding, as we were travelling to the Lakes on a fairly early train. I changed into my new suit in the choir's vestry – scene of so many changes in our play-acting days – and we scurried off amongst rice and confetti to begin our honeymoon.

In the train we shook out all the traces of our newly-weddedness, and arrived at the hotel trying to look like a staid old married couple.

There were drought notices all over the hotel, asking that water should be used very sparingly. Actually our wedding day was the last day of a long, dry spell. We went for a walk and then returned to the hotel for dinner.

As we were changing we heard voices through the open window. H. said, 'I'm sure I know that voice.' Sure enough there was a spinster lady, at whose house he'd spent a holiday, sitting with two cronies on a bench under the window. They were sitting at a table when we went into the dining room. Looking up the lady in question was most surprised and thrilled to see H. again. He introduced me as his wife.

'But I didn't know you HAD a wife!' she exclaimed.

'She's rather new,' he added.

'Oh, a bride! A bride! How lovely, a bride!' went up a chorus from the three old dears. I blushed profoundly, as was my wont, and was further embarrassed when, on leaving the dining room at the same time as the ladies they lined up on one side and insisted that I should go first.

'Make way for the bride,' they said. 'Oh yes, the bride must go first.' I needn't have taken all that trouble over the confetti and rice.

The rest of the honeymoon it never stopped raining.

H. had a fortnight's leave and we had decided to spend the last few days of it in our new home. It was soon apparent that Eric had summed up our landlady accurately. She wanted the rent, but not our presence. If she knew I was likely to be preparing a meal she saw to it that there was never a gas ring she wasn't using herself. The fact that H. took a cold bath every morning annoyed her. If friends came and the piano was played she turned up the radio in her room so loudly that the walls vibrated.

As they had only one fuel store and I used an electric fire excepting at the weekends, it had been arranged that our rent should include the kindling and fuel for that. She hid the sticks so that I couldn't light a fire.

A short time after H's departure the lady of the house was obliged to take a job. She then made it even more apparent that she didn't want me. I found I couldn't make my electric fire work and discovered she was switching off the power at the mains before catching her early bus. Before she began her job there had been signs of her prying into my drawers and cupboards. H. and I exchanged letters daily, and after reading mine at breakfast I always left it ready to answer with the fountain pen lying diagonally across it. Three days in succession I noticed that the pen had been moved and left at the side of the letter. That put the lid on it. I'd had Denys and Doug for a midday meal on Sunday and not been able to cook the meal until after they'd had to leave. They had echoed all that Eric thought about the lady of the house, and eaten cold food with as good a grace as possible. The letter business was the last straw. I wrote a letter myself and put it in the next morning's envelopes. 'Any more signs of petty interferences in my affairs and I shall take the matter further.'

For a week she scuttled out before I came down and waited outside in the porch for her bus time. In the evenings, she disappeared, presumably to her mother's and came back late at night. She'd obviously read the letter. But I couldn't stay there. I was used to a happy, good-natured family. Tom and his wife invited me to make my home with them, and found someone willing to store my furniture. It was a climb down, but it was heaven to be living with people who cared for one, to come home to marvellous meals and to laughing and singing.

Friends of H's who were renting a house near the station to which he was attached, invited me for Christmas. They were out for Christmas Day itself and H. and I had the house to ourselves. We had an enjoyable time at the Mess Dance, but behind it all I was very gloomy. H. had been warned of a posting, but he didn't know where. It could have been overseas. In the event he was sent to Douglas on the Isle of Man. At Easter I joined him there for about ten days. Life was a little bit more relaxed there than on the mainland. As a holiday resort there were flats to be had, and after Easter we decided to try and rent one from the end of the summer term. Other officers' wives seemed to think I was a bit odd to be doing my job still instead of following H. round. I wasn't sure that an aimless life would appeal to me, but I could see that a marriage was not easy to hold together indefinitely with the sort of arrangement we had.

When I told Miss T. I was resigning she was very sad about it. We had always got on very well together and I had kept up the standard of work well at the mission school. My mixed little flock had some real country children as well as those living on the fringe of the town. It was exciting to see their extreme shyness breaking down and to get them talking fluently and enjoying their work. Two such children came from a farm. Stanley was a bad stutterer and Margaret extremely thick in the head, and slow of speech. There was only an eight months' gap between their ages, which seemed very strange. However, when Margaret was asked tactfully about their relationship – for she did all the bossing although she was the younger – her reply was, 'Miss, 'e's me ooncle!'

The tallest boy amongst them was Derek Rohan. He was the son of middle-aged parents, and the mother hung over the school wall and devoured him with her eyes. He was an intelligent, but very mournful child, and to my amusement the other children called him Derek Groan. On Friday afternoons I let them think of what they would like to do, as long as all the week's work was completed. The girls liked to act, and would spend their playtimes practising a play. The boys were very lazy, excepting Derek. One Friday, however, they announced that they had a play to act. Poor Derek was the only one who knew his part. He kept growling the lines at the other boys, who were too bedazzled by their splendour as actors to remember they were supposed to speak. In the end, poor Derek leapt from one boy to the other, said the lines for him, and then went to his own place and carried on with his own part. The other boys didn't give a hoot, but the girls, all keyed up to see the boys in action at last, were shrieking with merriment before Derek turned to me mournfully and said, 'That's the end, Miss.'

They were all different, and as I had half of them for two years I got to know them very well. There were two bright little girls, bosom friends and yet the greatest rivals over their work. However many sums one did the other kept open a jealous eye and tried to do better. Needless to say they leapt on ahead of the others, and were a shining example to point to in respect of neatness as well as accuracy. The trouble came when one was ill and would not stay at home. She confided in the end that she couldn't stay in bed, '. . . else Celia will get in front.'

One little boy went berserk when his father was called up. His mother said he was quite out of control at home, and his work went to pot completely. To my very great distress he flew at my little song bird, a delightful happy little boy, and broke his arm. This meant a visit from Miss T. and a great hoo-hah. It was difficult to know how to help him. Drawing was his strong point, and in the end I tried to build up his shattered ego by complimenting him on his illustrations when his written work was beyond the pale. I allowed him to take his book round and show the other children. They were duly impressed and praised him. He began to calm down and attempt to make his written work measure up to his drawings. I told him he'd have to be the man at home now and help his mother and his young brother whilst Dad was away.

They confided their home worries and I heard of other dads who'd been killed or taken prisoner.

I was sorry to part with them at the end of the school year, and to say goodbye to all my old colleagues down at the main school. Sarina decided to retire from teaching when I left. Her father had bought a fancy goods and tobacconists's business for her brother, but he needed someone with him all the time. Sarina decided to throw in her lot with him. She was, in fact, an excellent business woman, and kept the business alive through difficult times until her own health failed some fifteen or so years later. We always kept in touch, and my first Christmas parcel was always a neatly wrapped, useful present from Sarina.

H. had succeeded in renting an attractive flat overlooking Douglas Bay and was impatient that I should join him as soon as possible. I packed in my canteen and hospital library jobs, began a round of farewells and then had a telegram to say H. had another posting. I was shattered, but heard in a few days that he had been moved to Northern Ireland.

It was not so easy to find accommodation there, but within a week or two I had news that his landlady had found a bungalow for us, and I joined him there in September. A colonel and his batman had been in residence before us, and the kitchen floor was filthy. I scrubbed it in vain for the few weeks of our stay there. The lounge and main bedroom were attractive. The small dining-room had a chimney which poured smoke back into the room and covered my washing with smuts, but it was our first home together in any real sense. We had a mad little kitten to prove we could please ourselves. We attacked the creeping buttercup in the garden with great resolution and looked forward to a long stay there.

The people were very friendly, and I was asked to form a Toc H.L.W.H. group, as some ladies running a canteen would like to belong to Toc. H. They were a merry crowd, and the people at the church invited me to tea and coffee, so that I felt involved very quickly.

H. had to travel to small units of the R.A.F. scattered round the northern counties, and when he was out for the night I felt rather bereft. I was, in fact, terrified when large black slugs began to appear on the bathroom floor. Most creatures I could tolerate, but not large black slugs.

However, seven weeks after my arrival H. received yet another posting. He suggested that I should stay in the bungalow and travel to join him later. I didn't fancy a wartime sea-crossing alone and I didn't fancy an indefinite stay with only the mad kitten and the appalling slugs for company. 'We'll stick together now I've given up my job,' was my attitude.

It was obvious that quarters would be waiting for him, but not for me. The posting was to Beechbeck in Derbyshire to a large trainer station. He was to be acting Senior Medical Officer in charge of sick quarters there, and he had a staff waiting to dance attendance on him.

Naturally he was worried about where I would stay. We changed trains at a market town some miles from Beechbeck, and decided to look for a hotel room there so that I was sure of a bed. We didn't know whether Beechbeck itself was more than two houses and a farm.

It looked at first as if no bed was to be had in the market town, but after some enquiring we found a pub with very limited residential accommodation, and I booked for three nights, hoping to get nearer to the sick quarters by the end of that time.

We'd spent a wakeful, miserable night crossing from Ireland and had been served with an appalling dried-egg breakfast at the only hotel which would let us in at nine o'clock in the morning. H. left me with all my baggage and departed to see what R.A.F. Beechbeck had in store for him. I had a meal and then went to see a Ralph Lynn and Tom Walls film before turning in for the night. When I returned to the pub the landlady said my husband had been trying to get me on the phone. He rang again to tell me that the first thing he'd seen on walking out of Beechbeck station was a sizeable hotel. He'd gone straight in and managed to book a room for me for a week or two. They were expecting me the next day. The hotel was only a mile from the 'drome and I could prospect from there for more permanent accommodation. I was overjoyed, and within twenty-four hours I walked through heaps of fallen leaves to the door of the Beechbeck Station Hotel.

The stink of stale cigarette smoke and sour beer assailed my nostrils as I penetrated the gloomy interior, but my bedroom was spacious and pleasant and an old Irish lady made me very welcome and chatted away to me in the dining room. I learned that she had gone there first as a permanent resident, but she did useful jobs about the place to help to pay for her keep.

That evening H. came to see how I'd settled in. By that time the place was swarming with R.A.F. personnel and their wives. The officers soon spotted H.'s badge and addressed him as Doc. and we were immediately drawn into the circle of the young pilots who were to train the newcomers. In the main they were the spoilt sons of well-to-do families, who had learned to fly for a lark before the war.

They were high-spirited dare-devils some of them, and their wives enjoyed living it up and being spoilt by the men.

The next day I began hunting for a place within the 'drome area, so that H. could live out. He had to be on the phone and within easy reach of Sick Quarters.

The little market town was packed with evacuees before the R.A.F. station was opened. I knocked on doors and enquired everywhere, but it was a disheartening task.

At one house I was told that there might be a chance of getting in at Bog End Farm. The farmer's wife took in summer visitors and it was in the middle of the 'drome area. My spirits rose as I trudged up a fantastically steep hill to look for the place.

I went into the farmyard and knocked on one of the doors of the farmhouse. A man's voice called, 'Come in,' and I went into the kitchen and saw Bill Jones sitting by the fire. He had a red friendly face and blue eyes. Two stout sticks leaning against his chair explained why he hadn't come to the door.

'Well, what can Ah dew fer yew, Missis?' he asked quite kindly. I began my tale apologetically, as by this time I felt very guilty about trying to squeeze into the overcrowded little town.

'Oh, well, yew'll 'ave to wait for Missis,' he said. 'She do let rewms and C.O.'s been here for a while, like. But 'e's gone now, an' I thowt she'd let rewms to an officer and his wife, but they've never been. She's nobbut down at neighbours if you'd like to wait.'

I sat down and let my eye wander round the cheerless place. There were no curtains at the window and nothing on the red brick floor, but a small rug immediately in front of the fire. Under the window was an old shallow sink. Pink had flaked from the walls, leaving green patches here and there. An open door revealed a walk-through dairy with stone slabs. A big gap under the door to the yard allowed the wind to whistle across the floor towards another door on the opposite side. A battered table and six old chairs and a very cluttered up old chest of drawers behind Bill's chair completed the furnishings.

I wondered what sort of rooms the C.O. and his lady had occupied, and my heart sank. But beggars can't be choosers, and it was in the 'drome area and on the telephone. I watched the yard entrance for the return of Mrs

Jones – the lady whose presence was all-important at Bog End.

Eventually an untidy middle-aged woman entered the farmyard. Her expression gave the impression that she was not a happy woman. Her coat was flying open and her greying black hair was wisping out from a loose knot. She was about as attractive as her kitchen, and my hopes sank more deeply.

However, when Bill had introduced us her expression changed to one of interest. 'Yer might's well 'ave 'em. The'others 'aven't come,' she sniffed. 'Come and 'ave a look at rooms, Mrs Moss – first come first served.'

She led the way through the dairy to another passage leading from a door nearer the entrance to the farm to three doors and a staircase. On the way we went by another room which she introduced as 'Th' little sittin' rewm'. That, I gathered, was the family sitting room, used at Christmas but piled high with every sort of object in the meantime. At the far end of the passage a door on the left gave entrance to 'the C.O.'s sitting room'. It had two windows, a patterned stone floor mainly covered by a fairly new carpet, a piano, table, chairs and a settee. The curtains were in a parlous state, but it was explained that the wooden shutters were closed at night, and a log fire made. 'It gets quite cosy,' Connie assured me.

'Th'bedrewm's up these stairs,' she said, going through another door on the far side of the room, which led to a porch and the front of the house. The 'best' stairs led from there to the two bedrooms which were let to visitors in peace time. They were over their respective sitting rooms. The C.O.'s bedroom was much more cheerless than the room downstairs. The curtains were little more than rags, but there was a double bed and a wardrobe and dressing-table. A drab, narrow, curtainless bathroom overlooked the farmyard and the passage to that led also to the four bedrooms and the back staircase used by the family and the maid. It was a much bigger house than one would have guessed from the yard. The two rooms looked onto the garden and a very boggy meadow. 'Sick quarters is up there,' said Connie, pointing to a group of temporary buildings about a quarter of a mile away. 'Th'doctor could soon be home from there. C.O. found it very convenient here, and main camp is further away than Sick Quarters.'

We discussed terms and I decided to take the plunge. Bill seemed very pleased when we returned to the kitchen. He had been joined by a black-haired young giant in his early twenties and a younger lad, not so sturdily built, in his late 'teens'. They were introduced as Roger and Stan, the two sons. I was to get to know them very well in the next twelve months.

We moved in the next day and began a new chapter in our lives.

CHAPTER EIGHT

BOG END

Born and bred a townie, H. was thrilled to be living on a farm. What the fare lacked in variety it made up in substance, and we were not limited to rations, excepting in sugar and tea – neither of which was a hardship. We discovered two years later that Connie bought all our rations in our name and never paid the bills. Her attitude over financial arrangements was unpredictable. We paid an 'all-in' rate by cheque once a fortnight, but the same cheques were liable to be blowing about the corridor floor when she pulled something from a coat pocket. The door was open quite often, and the coats hung there for all comers to see. The cheques were cashed in time, but no one ever knew Connie's time. Certainly, I heard from the proprietor of the shop where she'd bought our rations that they had never been paid for.

The farm belonged to Connie and was rented to Bill and his sons at the highest rent in Beechbeck. The men worked very hard and were sound farmers, but they refused to pay for any fundamental improvements – land drains and so on. Connie was equally adamant that she wouldn't fork out, so the front of the house was in a quagmire and the cellar was full of water.

Our fire was not lit until midday, and I found the room deadly cold. By the time H. came in for his one o'clock meal the fire had been going long enough to take the chill off. When the shutters were closed in the evening and logs piled on the fire it became more than cosy.

I used to go out and saw logs in order to get my circulation going, or walk into Beechbeck and stagger back up the hill. I polished the bits of the floor not covered by the carpet until they were like glass. Sitting was out of the question before the fire was lit.

The piano had not been tuned for years and had suffered from cold and damp. Half the notes were dead.

Much of the winter there was thick fog, and it was pressing gloomily against the windows for days on end.

My bones began to creak, and I was suddenly smitten by lumbago. Everyone thought that funny excepting me.

The first night of night-flying the planes headed straight for our bedroom. The noise was hideous, and in the middle of the night there was an almighty crackle and crash, and there in the meadow a few yards from our window, was the wreck of a plane. It had hit a tree on the other side of the road and been diverted, otherwise it would have hit our bedroom. It does not require much imagination to understand my state of mind when the wind was such that the planes took off from that particular runway. In addition I was at all times an extremely light sleeper. Any night flying meant a very bad night, but it was impossible to get to sleep on 'our' nights.

Airmen are superstitious, and 'one crash usually means three' was accepted as a commonplace. After a crash the squadron leaders on duty for the next night-flying session would pray for fog to come down to prevent it. My husband and his staff had the ghastly job of seeking for parts of bodies – a hand here and a leg there – in order to complete some sort of body to put in a coffin for the bereaved parents to follow at funerals when the very worst happened. He would come back in the small hours very white and shaken.

There was of course the lighter side. I was thrown into the company of other officers' wives at dances and so on. They came from all over the country, and all sorts of backgrounds. The most striking looking and gayest was, alas, a nymphomaniac, and much too fond of gin. Her little boy was left in the care of a village girl more often than not, and her flirtations with her husband's colleagues were absolutely blatant. If invited out to tea she would ask if she might bring her latest with her. Her poor husband was last heard of volunteering for particularly dangerous operational missions, hoping, one assumed, that the time would come when he was not obliged to come back to see his little son neglected and his ravishing wife ogling someone else.

The two of them were in fact the couple who had been offered our quarters at Bog End, but they ended up in a very beautiful old house which they rented, furnished, with one of H.'s junior M.O.s. They had drinking parties, and the lovely furnishings suffered. An overdraft was an essential part of their economy.

My Methodist background made that sort of behaviour difficult to understand. My mother had brought up seven of us on the slenderest resources and never owed a penny. The odd glass of sherry or port to mark an occasion was all that was really acceptable in the way of alcohol, and the terrible lives lived by the families who were dependent on drunken fathers or husbands was plain enough for anyone to see, even in our small town.

At the mess dances drinking to excess was all part and parcel of 'having a good time'. I liked the people sober, but I hated to see them standing in pools of spilt beer or wrecking the place and carrying on with other men's wives. It seemed to me that when the war was over so many of them would have to face broken marriages and unpaid debts.

On one occasion all leave was cancelled at short notice. There was to be a major all-out push against the enemy. All those about to go on leave were furious, and they consoled themselves by getting stoned. Amongst them was a charming girl from a good family. She was engaged to be married and probably hoped to meet her fiancé whilst on leave.

As it happened she was plied with drink and subsequently made pregnant by a man for whom she cared nothing and whose name she probably didn't know. It was another of the tragic problems brought to H. She came and wept bitterly at what havoc one night's unaccustomed drinking had caused to her life, and was desolate at the thought of having to tell her fiancé and the parents who had been so happy about her engagement.

There was one well remembered night when I danced for the first and last time with an earl! He happened to be the C.O. at the time, a man even more shy than my husband and still a bachelor.

There was thick snow on the ground when the invitations went out to all the officers to attend the sergeants' mess dance. Their mess was some distance away, and I put on sheepskin boots and as many warm clothes as possible. On arrival I could see no one I knew. None of the other officers' wives had turned up, and no other officer excepting the shy C.O. The concrete floor was not conducive to stylish dancing, nor were my sheepskin boots, but there it is, I danced with the earl. The poor man had to ask me. However, he didn't have to be a brilliant conversationalist. I did my best, pathetic as that was, and he broke the intervening gaps with the odd banal remark. I doubt whether he saw the humour of the situation. For me it just made the three mile trudge through the snow to the cheerless hut worthwhile. I'd danced with an earl, come what may!

We had met a vet and his doctor wife, who were in very attractive rooms at a nearby farm. The rooms were furnished by an estate agent with beautiful antiques. When we were invited there to dinner one evening I was green with envy. Our hosts laughed and said they could imagine our quarters, but they knew they were very lucky. They had heard of their rooms because the vet was stationed with the Re-Mounts at the estate where the owner of the furniture worked in peacetime.

We invited them back, and of course needed the help of Connie in providing a meal for them.

Connie knew only too well what a contrast there was between their rooms and ours. The curtains were her greatest concern, and on the day of the expected visit she suddenly announced, 'I've 'ad some material for new curtains for 'ere since before war, but I'm not very good with sewin' now. Would you like to 'elp make 'em for tonight, Missis?'

I couldn't refuse, but time was very short. She fetched the material and we measured it against the windows. It was just long enough. The sewing machine was dug out of 'little sittin' room' and cotton and tapes hunted up. I set to, my eye on the clock, knowing that it was a race against time. I had one finished and the other begun when it was zero hour. Connie had removed the raggy old ones and laid the table. The fire was roaring away. H. took the one curtain and had got it in place when Connie came in and said, 'They're in the road, finish top and we'll put unhemmed bottom behind sofa.' I rushed through and handed the curtain to H. A knock on the 'front' door by the sunken porch announced our guests. 'Go and keep them at bay for a minute,' said H. climbing onto the settee.

I went and dragged open the ill-fitting door. 'Hello,' I said, 'did you notice all the lovely snowdrops?' I passed them and went into the freezing night.

'We're not bothered about the snowdrops. Let us in. It's perishing cold out here and we know you're still putting up the curtains, but never mind.' My Scottish guest enjoyed the joke and I was glad to get back to the log fire. H. was sitting down as if nothing had happened and Connie was all smiles. We ate a big meal and roasted ourselves and then explained that the bottom hem was waiting to be done on the part behind the settee. 'We're greatly honoured,' they declared.

Bill, having seen me hard at work on the sewing machine, decided my talents were being wasted. He was an outsize figure and Connie couldn't buy him comfortable shirts. The ones he wore were in tatters.

'Why don't y'ask Mrs Moss t'elp make them shirts Ah've been waitin' for for tew year?' he asked Connie. 'She's got fine little fingers she could show y'ow to go on. Couldn't you, Mrs Moss?'

'I'm afraid shirts are beyond me,' I replied. 'What about the collars and so on?'

'Oh, Ah, Ah've got bought neck-pieces right size,' said Connie, 'but I daren't dew cuttin' out. Materials been waitin' in little sittin' rewm since before war.'

It was a challenge I couldn't refuse. Connie had no shirt pattern, but I used one of Bill's old relics and walked round the kitchen table pinning it onto the stout flannel, with all the family watching entranced.

'Now,' said Bill, 'if yew make one and the Missis watches, she can make th'other if yew cut it out.' It was not a masterpiece, but it was a warm, whole shirt, and Bill was delighted. I'm afraid he was very rude about Connie's 'gert, rough 'ands' and the button holes they made. I know that she had been quite the young lady before her marriage and had done a lot of embroidery, but her sight was poor, and she never wore gloves. I'm afraid the lady in her had been lost in years of disillusion and work.

During bleakest February, when, in spite of the hundreds of snowdrops, fog, snow and sleet persisted, Bill went down with phlebitis. His crippling arthritis made his movements very slow at the best of times, but he did cover a lot of work in the course of the day. In any case he was a mine of information and his two sons were used to acting under his instructions. With him upstairs things began to go very badly. There was a young fellow in the district who was willing to help at Bog End, but Connie disliked his politics. His mother came once a week to do a slatternly clean of the upstairs, but Connie tolerated her. The boys couldn't see that the politics of a neighbour mattered as long as he was willing to 'muck out th'cows.' Connie said she could do it and fell full length.

H. went down to breakfast one morning and then came back to the bedroom. 'Don't be in a hurry to get up today,' he said. 'The atmosphere downstairs is sulphuric. She says she's leaving them. Keep out of the way until things are quieter.'

When I did venture forth Connie was in the little sitting room speaking on the telephone. She came out and went to the bottom of the back staircase, just outside one of our doors. From there she addressed Bill, shouting so that her voice carried up the stairs, along a corridor and into his room. 'Ah've been on th'phone to th'lawyer an' 'e says Ah might'swell leave yer. Ah've not 'ad a 'appy day sin' we've been married. You can dew as yer please about gettin' that young communist then. Ah'm goin' up to fetch th'osses then Ah'm off, and good riddance!'

She stomped through the passage out into the yard and I saw her distracted figure walking along the road up to the field where the two horses were kept.

I then went quickly into the kitchen and prepared my own breakfast, and finding Stanley there unfed, cooked his as well.

'She says she's goin',' he told me. 'She's said it before, but she means it this time.' I said I thought she'd come round and asked where the maid was. 'Oh she's outside in th'milk 'ouse. Mam's given 'er th'sack. She's cryin' out there and daren't come in.' I told him to fetch the girl and suggested we had a meal as quickly as possible, but when the sound of the horses' hooves rang in the yard entrance the maid scuttled out again, and Stanley crammed bread in his pockets and left quickly.

I was washing up when Connie, having dealt with the horses, came into the kitchen. She ignored me and began to change her stockings by the fire. I commented on the miserable sleety morning. 'Adn't noticed it,' was all she said. She had indeed gone off for the horses with her unbuttoned coat flying in the wind and no gloves, as usual.

When she put on her good coat and a hat I knew she meant business, and she repeated to me what she'd said to poor Bill. ''E's a bad un. Ah should never 'ave 'ad 'im. Ah'm off. They can dew as they please then.'

She departed and I coaxed the miserable maid indoors again. She was from a poor family and Connie suspected her of spending her free time at the cottage of the whore who obliged some of the airmen. She did in fact steal some of my clothes and some of Connie's food eventually, but that is another story. I persuaded her that Connie didn't really mean to dismiss her for good, and got her to begin her normal duties. The uneven brick floor had to be washed every day, along with the stone slab floor in the dairy. (No wonder poor Bill was arthritic and young Stanley already showing signs of going the same way.)

I discussed what food was in the dairy and planned and prepared a good midday meal. Roger and Stanley came in and ate their food glumly. I took the first course upstairs to Bill and then ate mine. When I went up again for his empty plate the maid met me coming down again and handed me the plate with his pudding. On my speedy return with the sweet course Bill remarked, 'Yew was quick, Mrs Moss.'

'Oh, I was met half way,' I replied.

'Aye, so was I wunce,' he said, with deep meaning.

The day passed quietly and the boys came in for their tea. 'No sign of 'er yet?'

'No,' I answered. They rang up her brother and sister and anyone she might have gone to, but they drew a blank every time. When the fog settled again they became really anxious.

H. and I retired to our room, which was always the cosiest place at Bog End by the evening. We wondered what our position would be if our unorthodox landlady had really skedaddled and left the three men to cope without her.

H. was reading and I was weaving when footsteps in the passage and a familiar sniffing announced the wanderer's return. She always knocked and entered our room without waiting for an invitation. In she came, her best hat at a rakish angle and her face wreathed in smiles. She was holding two rather nice expensive necklaces. 'Now, doctor,' she said, 'if yew was our Roger, w'ich o' these would yer give to 'is Mary for an engagement present?' We discussed the merits of both necklaces and then she confided, 'Ah've 'ad a luvley day. Been ter th'jeweller's for th'day. Ah was at school with 'is wife an' she's asked me many a time ter go. Ah decided to go this mornin'. Luvley day. Ah shall tell our Roger yer like this one,' she added, as she returned to the bosom of her family.

A discreet tap two hours later was followed by Stanley's face peeping round our door. He was a rare visitor in our room, but it had been a rare day and required a suitable requiem. He said with his eyes twinkling with relief and amusement, 'Leave 'em alone an' they'll come 'ome – waggin' their tails a'hint 'em.' He wagged his finger very descriptively and went up to the room he shared with his dad.

Before the winter was out I was a regular visitor to the room, massaging oil of wintergreen into their stiff and painful shoulders. I had become an expert administering the same treatment to my spouse. My own bones objected to living in such a damp and chilly place. 'We must get out of here before next winter,' H. said.

I helped Roger catch the lambs when they had strayed from their mothers, and listened with delight to Bill's description of the cows when they were let out into the yard for an airing. He loved them all, and especially the one with udders 'soft and silky like a lass's blouse.' I often wondered about his courting days and if the poor relationship was the result of parents' interference in their early days. Connie had an enormous sister and a gigantic brother. As children they had been very spoilt by an over-indulgent mother, who always referred to them collectively as 'th' little darlin's'. Bill used to tell me tales about them, as we stood watching the cows, and if the enormous sister called in her equally enormous car – almost tipping the vehicle over as she got in and out – he would lift his stick to his mouth and say to me out of the corner, 'Look out. 'Ere comes one of th' little darlin's.' He was a naughty old man. I had such a job to keep a straight face.

Bill and Connie seemed to care nothing for each other's happiness. He had a few ducks which delighted to hide in the reeds round the pond when it was their 'locking-up time'. He had a very special clacking call which usually beguiled them out of their hiding and to his feet before it was quite dark. Connie kept a few hens in a very sketchy way. Their home was a hut in a barbed wire enclosure half-way down the meadow where the plane had crashed. The barbed-wire was to keep the young heifers away. They (the heifers) were a very curious lot – that is to say curious – 'nosey', not curious 'peculiar'. They seemed to think that the wrecked plane was a source of great interest, and usually gathered near it.

But to get back to the barbed wire – Connie went down to feed her hens and look for eggs only when the spirit moved her, which was never in the very worst weather. They were a wretched-looking lot of creatures, and very rarely laid an egg. Connie bought dozens of eggs from Roger's fiancée's mother. However, visiting her own hens, albeit not religiously, told a tale on Connie's vestures, for as she bent to get under the barbed wire the same bit of material was plucked at each time. She had therefore a hole in the seat of her dress, and her thick combinations were underneath for all the world to see.

One morning the bleak kitchen was graced by a beautiful rose which Stanley had worn in his buttonhole at a dance the night before. He loved flowers, and had put it in a glass in the kitchen window.

Bill, sitting in his usual place by the fire, gave me a sly wink and addressed his wife. 'Ah've 'eerd tell as some women wears pretty things un'erneath their dresses. Ah'm sick o' seein' your combinations threw yon 'ole in back of your dress. If you'd like ter pass me that rose our Stanley's left in th'winder Ah'll 'broider it in th'ole for yer.'

I retired hastily through the dairy to hide my face, but his sally had the desired effect. She wore a different dress the next day.

I was asked to help run the W.V.S. Canteen in Beechbeck and there I met an old farmer's widow who told me endless tales about Beechbeck's history and the gossip about the families in the district. We were on an early duty together and there was often a long time between our preparing for the rush and the first sight of uniformed figures coming through the door.

One tale she told was of how Connie's family had come by their money

– apparently by the guile of an ancestor who had been a butler to a very wealthy man. It was considered 'bad' money by the locals, who swore that no happiness would go with it. Certainly the thousands inherited by 'th'little darlin's' didn't seem to have brought much happiness. If Bill had married for money he'd had no comfort from it. I shall never know. I never heard him speak with any affection of Connie, but from his remark on the day when she 'left' them I assumed their first-born was on his way before any banns were announced. Connie told me it snowed on their wedding day, and she thought that a bad omen, as it was in May. But I've seen snow flurries in July in those parts, so snow in May was no great wonder. The old farmer's widow told me Connie used to walk about the hills with her baby in her arms looking like a wild creature from a Brontë novel. I can believe it, and yet she could show great affection and kindness when she felt that way, and was always very fond of H.

I sorted through bags of rotting potatoes to find the sound ones for her, and gathered the gooseberries from devilishly prickly bushes. I must say I was a bit staggered when she charged me for two pounds of the said gooseberries to make into jam with our extra sugar ration.

But H.'s determination to be out before another winter led to my scanning the local paper by the end of the summer. Strangely enough, someone was offering two rooms without food or service, and I went to see them. They were out of the town on the opposite side to the 'drome, but H. had two junior doctors by that time, and could live a bit further away. One junior was unmarried and living in sick quarters, so we weren't as tied.

Connie was very upset when we moved, and confided to someone, 'It weren't doctor, you know. It were missus!' I think H.'s unfailing politeness was a salve to her troubled spirit. For thirty years we have exchanged Christmas greetings and we visited fairly recently after a very long gap. Connie's daughter-in-law has made a very attractive and comfortable home of Bog End. The farm has all the latest equipment. Stanley now looks the image of his father thirty years ago, but without the bitter twist to his humour and without the tell-tale stout walking sticks. Connie in her eighties still seems to be half in this world and half in an unhappy one of her own imagining. Once she had placed us, her eyes are bad now, she seemed pleased to see us and to accept a lift to visit an old friend in a neighbouring town. Sitting beside th'doctor she came out of her dream world and talked quite warmly about her grandchildren. Her prematurely-aged husband died many years ago.

CHAPTER NINE

PRIVATE SCHOOL AND PREGNANCY

We moved from Bog End to the Manse when the leaves were falling. It seemed that we were destined to be settling into a new home every autumn.

After the depressing view across the boggy meadow with the wrecked plane, our view from the big bay of the manse was breathtaking. The ground swept down to a river with an attractive bridge to the left of the scene. On the other side it rose steeply to a wonderful backcloth of woods, meadows and small farmsteads. A fine gaggle of geese moved in dignified procession down to the river every day. We were within cycling distance of some of the most beautiful scenery in Derbyshire. Back towards the town was an extremely steep hill, which dropped even more steeply to the market place. We still heard the planes, especially when they took off into the north, but they were not flying low over our bedroom.

The defects of the Manse lay in the paper thin carpets, large unshuttered, very draughty windows, and the very great difficulty in getting even reasonably warm. Away from the farm I was dependent on shopkeepers for food and had to try to make do on rations. H. had a good midday meal in the mess, which was a help, but I spent a lot of time trying to make a substantial evening meal out of very little.

I missed the animals at the farm. Glad indeed I was not to have to fetch coal from the store next to the bull's shed. I had christened him Gustav. He was a fearsome creature, and rattled the padlocked door noisily and restlessly by the hour. I could hear him snorting menacingly as I hastily filled the scuttle. The old sheepdog was not afraid of him, and on one occasion when Gustav escaped to the meadow and was seen trying to push down a tree the old dog fetched him back very skilfully. I loved him, and always made a fuss of him. He was not allowed indoors excepting during thunder storms. He was then reduced to a pitiful bundle of nerves, and his master winked a blind eye as he slunk in through the kitchen door and went to his little refuge in a store room containing the men's Wellington boots. He was so ashamed of his cowardice. Normally he came round for a fuss along with old Grandma, the veteran of the farm cats. I saved the bacon rinds for her. She was a moth-eaten old girl, but proved her prowess by producing a single kitten whilst we were at Bog End. Her hussy of a daughter also produced a family at the same time, and she was off with the toms again in no time, leaving poor Grandma to suckle her twins as well as her own kitten.

From my window at the Manse I watched the geese go down to the water every day, but on one occasion when I went visiting on the other side of the valley the huge gander put his head down and hissed at me. I didn't trespass on their territory again.

An advertisement in the local paper for a teacher had attracted my eye before leaving the farm. I went to see the principal of the tiny private school and in the end agreed to go. The salary was infinitesimal, but it just covered my lunches at a modest café and left me a few shillings over. My main concern was to be with children again. They were, of course, the children of the well-to-do families – many of them very charming, but spoilt. I asked about the teaching methods and was met by a blank stare. The courses were really set for children being taught in their own homes, and the idea was that what the teacher said the children repeated. They could talk, but that was the lot. The standard of reading and number was appallingly bad. Singing games consisted of musical bumps with much shrieking, and their play break was spent in keeping to the paths in the garden. I thought of the marvellously planned and graded physical education syllabus I had used in my old schools and of the high standards in reading, composition and number attained. These children of the 'privileged' Beechbeck families were having a very raw deal.

I was given the four and five-year olds and I took them into the cloakroom and gave them a blitz on reading. They were intelligent and were soon romping away as keen as mustard. But that didn't suit the principal. Her seven-year-old daughter couldn't read, and eight-year-olds were still stumbling over small words. I found it hard to believe. She took me from the little ones and said in her system it was not an advantage to read before eight years old. I was asked to cope with the older children's arithmetic. It was shocking. The poor kids hadn't been grounded in anything, and were completely at sea. I said it was a waste of time to give them work they couldn't understand. They needed to go back to the beginning and be soundly grounded, given mental arithmetic every day to sharpen them up and build up their confidence. In English they were doing Shakespeare's *King John* from the original!

It was the principal's habit to make out on the reports that the children were naturally slow. I stayed there for a year, hammering away at essentials and getting very good results once the children had gained their confidence, but I was constantly moved from one group to another. I bought some suitable music and built up a repertoire of songs and singing games, but with children from four to ten in one room it was far from ideal. I went home grousing and before the end of the summer had a second miscarriage. H. pushed me to pack it in. I loved the children, but the principal was given to black moods and victimization of the odd child she considered not quite from the right drawer. I'd had the headmistress of the local church school begging me to go and take her infants' class. I knew I'd have a room to myself there and a free hand, so in the end I agreed. The news of my departure upset the principal and the parents of the children, but I stuck to my guns. My last week or two the principal asked if she might study my methods in reading and number. She had not trained at all, but taken on the school in order to get the flat that went with it. It hurt her feelings very much that I should leave to go to a 'local' school. If I'd left to have a baby that would have been accepted. I was sorry to leave the children I'd grown so fond of, but knew that there were many more children with no qualified teacher waiting at the church school.

The headmistress there was a voluble, rather overpowering woman at first sight, but I found her a most helpful and appreciative person to work for, and a very compassionate and capable teacher and friend. In one class I had more than twice the number of the whole school I'd just left. There was the little Cockney evacuee, so intelligent and so neglected. He lived on an outlying farm with a single woman reputed to be mad. He came wearing a pyjama top as a shirt and it was never washed. His head was filthy and I couldn't tell him not to keep coming out to have his sums marked. My praise meant such a lot to the lonely little fellow, but at six he was too young to wash his own hair. I caught lice from him and had to ask the school nurse to exclude him until he was cleaned up. I went nearly crackers until I'd got my own head cleaned, I might say.

A local children's home wished a group of very young children on the school. It included one little Sylvia – a veritable belle of St Trinian's. Her language was appalling, and her social habits disgusting. When I tried to discipline her she spat at me and swore so that the other children's eyes popped out. I asked for her removal on the grounds that she was really under school age and mentally defective. A poor haunted-looking woman came down from the home to say she was sure she wasn't mentally defective – she could sing like an angel. Had I heard her sing, 'Jesus bids us shine'? She had indeed a most tuneful and sweet voice, but her language would have made a convict blush, and I wasn't prepared to be wiping a four-year-old's spit from my eye when I'd thirty-eight or more other children to teach.

One nervous little boy was always wanting to 'leave the room'. On one occasion he put up his hand just as I told them to put their hands together to sing grace before going home. I whispered, 'Just wait a moment, Johnny.' But poor Johnny gave a strangulated, 'It's toming, it's toming – oh, it's tome!' and indeed it had – all down his shoes and socks and in a pool on the floor. We all make mistakes. After that it was a case of 'Fling wide the gates' when his hand began to rise – grace or no grace!

The occupants of the manse were obliged to move on the following summer, and we had been invited to rent two unfurnished rooms in a lovely old house up a very steep bank behind the school. So autumn again sent us settling into new surroundings, this time with our own furniture and a much greater degree of physical comfort. Just before we moved I thought I might be pregnant again. After a positive test H. gave me injections and at long last it looked as if I might be lucky. We had been married over three years and although H. had not been keen on having children at first he was now as keen as I was. We kept it to ourselves in case I had another calamitous miscarriage.

It was marvellous to have our own things again and a good piano. We were above the most fog-bound level of the town and had a wonderful view of the beautiful church lying down by the little stream which gave Beechbeck its name.

I had begun my new job only a week or two when my pregnancy was established, and the old doctor in the town said he thought I should not teach after Christmas.

It seemed a shame to have to give up the new job so soon, but I daren't fly in the face of the advice of H. and the old GP. Miscarriages are shattering and I was beginning to hate my stupid body for not being able to reproduce. I would be over twenty-eight by the time the baby was due, and that was plenty late enough for a first baby.

It came about then that almost as soon as I'd got into a really satisfactory routine with my new children we were preparing for Christmas, and my departure was imminent. The Christmas party there was so much more enjoyable than the parties at the private school. The children were obviously very happy and appreciative, but there was none of the wilful shrieking and constant showing off which had characterized the children from the well-to-do homes.

The headmistress was very sorry, but understood my position. She would not visit me in my new quarters at Sweet Meadow, as she had no great opinion of my new landlady, but we did keep in touch.

Sweet Meadow had been a farmhouse, was about two hundred years old and very charming. The second storey was not used as the floorboards were rotten. We had two rooms, on the first storey, and the use of the bathroom.

I had first visited Sweet Meadow when trying desperately to find rooms for a friend with two babies. She had been obliged to leave London because of the flying bombs when her second baby was a few weeks old. However, Janice Pedley, the gay little wife at Sweet Meadow said she couldn't do with two babies there, but if H. and I would like to go she would empty two rooms for us and make a flat for herself and her husband downstairs. At that time I did not know that the minister and his wife would be moving the next year, and I had not accepted the offer, but by the autumn of 1944 it seemed too good a chance to ignore.

There had been other lavish offers of making a special kitchenette for us, but these didn't materialize. However, a big cupboard was fitted with an air brick and a double gas ring and a small deep sink replaced a wash basin under one of the windows. There was another window, a bay, with a beautiful view. It was a spacious room and made a comfortable living-room.

By this time all our old friends from the 'drome had moved on. H. was expecting an overseas posting anytime, but his senior at Group H.Q. knew of my pregnancy and that I had no parents, and I think he quite deliberately delayed things. R.A.F. Beechbeck was being run down, and if H. had stayed there he would have had to accept a drop in rank, so he was posted to a station in the south, and when that station folded up to another and yet another. It meant that I was about the last of the R.A.F. wives left in Beechbeck, and I missed my closest friend very much. She had had her first baby whilst I was at the manse, and we'd had a lot of fun together. We were the same age and both teachers, so we'd seen eye-to-eye in many ways. Unfortunately we lost touch. No doubt Freddie, her husband, was moved about a good deal.

As soon as H. had gone Janice's husband decided he didn't want a pregnant woman in the house, if they couldn't have children of their own he wasn't putting up with other people's, but Janice burst into tears and sent him to Coventry. I began to cast round desperately for unfurnished accommodation, and Janice told me to stop it – she wanted the dear little baby as much as I did. I stayed and things settled down a bit, but I felt I was living on quicksand.

No doubt as child substitutes, Janice had two little dogs – one a dear little Scottie and the other a terribly spoilt Peke. They were both bitches, and the trim little figure of Janice with the two little bitches fussing along beside her was a well-known sight in the town. Her husband was very deaf, a business man and a local man, and he had none of his wife's airs and graces. He was all for the quiet life, but she was all for bridge parties and cutting a dash in new rig-outs.

When both the bitches were on heat the Pedleys decided to take a holiday, leaving me in charge of them. Never having owned a bitch I was green enough to comply. Sweet Meadow was besieged by every hound for miles round. They included an enormous Alsatian from the house across the road, and it was hell let loose to try and air Janice's pets, or to try and emerge to do my shopping. It was also at this time that I discovered just what a dirty little so-and-so the peke was – much preferring to use the dining room carpet to the grass outside. I was not amused.

Janice had at one time had the old Irish lady from the Station Hotel living 'au pair', and she missed her ministrations. After a time she decided she must have a living-in maid in order to keep up her prestige. Domestic help was not easy to get, but she heard of someone who had been in service all her life and who was looking for a new home.

The spare bedroom next to ours was to be given her, and the old soul turned up. She was a character, if ever I met one; but Janice had got her heart's desire, although I could see that her spouse eyed the old lady dubiously.

Her first duty was to take early morning tea to Janice and Laurie, and then she was to see to the stove in the dining room. This latter was a new closed stove, whose character had not yet been tamed. It was difficult to light, and never gave out enough heat to warm the big, cold room.

At this time my baby was kicking violently and I woke very early. On Rebecca's first day at Sweet Meadow I was awakened even earlier by the most desperate choking and coughing from the spare bedroom. I toddled along and made a pot of tea, deciding that poor Rebecca would need oiling before her old wheels would turn. She accepted gratefully and I made a habit of it. It was some time later when I went downstairs and had occasion to go through the dining room. The Pedleys were sitting in stony silence eating a late breakfast – certainly not cooked to Janice's high standard. Poor Rebecca was on her knees doing battle with the stove. She never learned how to cope, and Mr Pedley resumed his muttering and grumbling over the job after a few days. Janice was really an excellent cook and had plenty of energy, and waiting for poor Rebecca to do jobs was not easy for her.

Another holiday was indicated – a longer one. Rebecca was invited to spring clean the house whilst they took a fortnight's holiday at an hotel. Something told me they would be back early. They had a very high standard of living, as Mr Pedley's business was a flourishing grocery concern, and I knew no hotel would measure up to Janice's standards of cooking, nor her husband's as far as quantity went.

However, they departed and I was left again with the two bitches and Rebecca. The latter saw it as a golden opportunity to bring Sweet Meadow up to the standard of a 'gentleman's house'. No one visiting saw it as anything else, but then, no one went into the cellars. They were lovely arched cellars and contained nothing but coal. I imagine Rebecca thought of cellars as repositories of wine. At any rate she would begin by scrubbing them clean and work her way upwards. To make her job easier when she began on the ground level she removed every vase and ornament, picture and so on and piled things on the bed and the dining table. After that she began on the cellars.

Pail after pail of hot soapy water she took down the narrow steps, and pail after pail of black sludge she brought up again. She trotted a dismal trail through the hall and dining room to the kitchen. She scrubbed and scrubbed for days, wearing herself out. 'I'll get it clean if it kills me. Call it a gentleman's house – with cellars like that!'

I began to get worried. A week fled by and she was still not satisfied. I had a card from Janice hinting that her husband was not comfortable at the hotel. I was sure my hunch was right and that they would come home early, but Rebecca would not listen to me. 'I shall be ready when they come. I've only the last three steps to scrub and then I can begin up here.' 'Up here' was by this time in a shocking state. The milkman put his head in at the kitchen window and nearly had a fit. Janice's pale blue and white emporium was grubby beyond recognition. I daren't insult the old soul by interfering beyond giving another solemn warning.

I was afflicted with phlebitis in my late pregnancy and spent some time sitting sewing on the terrace outside the downstairs rooms. I was there when I heard Janice call out, 'We're back. We decided to come home early.'

It was followed by an ominous silence then, 'Are you there, Nancy?'

'Coming,' I called and went indoors. Janice's expression was beyond description. Laurie was bringing in the cases and saw me before the state of the house registered with him. As Janice explained that they'd left the hotel because Laurie didn't like the food, Laurie, deaf as a post, was telling me they'd been turned out by the manager for grumbling so much.

'Where's Rebecca? What on earth has happened? I've never seen such a mess in all my life. I asked her to do the spring cleaning. I just can't believe it.' Janice bustled through to find the wretched Rebecca taking off her coarse scrubbing apron and trying to put in her teeth (kept, to Laurie's intense chagrin, in a cup in the kitchen excepting when she answered the door) and tie on her best apron and wash her hands all at once. The poor soul was weary to dropping point.

Laurie was still laughing at me at the thought of being turned out of a hotel. I think he felt a bit of a dog. When Janice returned I tried to justify the behaviour of poor Rebecca. 'She was beginning up here tomorrow. She really has been working like a nigger ever since you left.'

'She must be absolutely crazy,' was Janice's reaction. 'As soon as I can find someone to house her I shall get rid.'

Poor Rebecca! She further sealed her doom by eating the wrong fish one day. Janice had bought halibut for herself and Laurie and decided on cod or haddock for Rebecca, as the halibut seemed expensive. Old Rebecca decided to have her own meal early before serving theirs and she made a good meal of the halibut and took the other to them half an hour later. They were speechless with anger. Rebecca felt she couldn't please them, however hard she tried.

Janice heard of an eighty-year-old invalid who needed a resident housekeeper. Rebecca was hustled into a taxi with her belongings and bid godspeed.

After her departure the house began to run smoothly again, and Janice settled for a daily help. This time she did much better. The help was young and active and about Janice's build. This meant that she was able to wear Janice's cast-offs, and she handed over her clothing coupons in exchange. With these, and her own and most of her husband's, Janice was able to cut a dash when most of the ladies of Beechbeck were reduced to 'making do'.

No doubt when twenty years younger her face had matched her trim little figure, but in her fifties her teeth were bad and she rather resembled her fussy little peke, Diddley Doo. Hats were not on coupons and she was able to give full rein to her love of finery when shopping in the millinery departments, but on viewing the treasures in the cold light of Laurie's gaze the hats were sometimes found to have intrinsic faults. On one occasion she decided she had been diddled and rang up the store to complain. The boy who answered the phone didn't cover the mouthpiece before calling out to an assistant, 'Hey, John, there's an old hag on the phone wanting the hat department.' I must add that what the 'old hag' demanded next was to speak to the manager. 'I may be an old hag, but I'm not going to be called one by your ignorant assistants. You'd better sack that boy.' I've no doubt the lad had a flea in his ear. Poor Janice told the tale when her bosom friend and I joined her for coffee one morning. Vi Garret enjoyed the tale and gave me a sly wink. She was a good sport and a very generous woman. She had been married to a mean man, who had left her a wealthy widow. She loved fine clothes as much as Janice, but couldn't lay her hands on as many extra coupons. She told me that she always kept one specially nice dress 'for fear'.

'For fear of what?' I asked, quite puzzled.

'Oh, for fear someone asks me out for a special occasion.' In contrast to Janice she was a very popular woman, as she took great pleasure in giving money to worthy causes to make amends for her husband's stinginess.

Just as soon as VE day was over Vi decided she would be ready for peacetime and buy a car. She trotted down into town and bought a dashing little model and then came to Sweet Meadow to tell her exciting news. 'What do you think? I've bought a car and I'm going to have driving lessons!' Janice was furious. In less than twenty-four hours she and Laurie persuaded Vi that it was a silly step to take and that the proprietor of the garage was a rogue and sure to have done her down. Vi was very crestfallen, but Janice's word always carried in their little circle. 'Stop the cheque and cancel everything,' she counselled. 'If you don't hurry it will be too late.' She had her way. Vi's hopes were dashed, but within the week the two

Pedleys had taken a trip into Derby and bought a car. It was a near thing. Vi almost had the edge on her for once. I thought it was a very mean trick, but Beechbeck society laughed and said it was quite typical.

When my phlebitis had subsided my last few weeks of pregnancy were coloured by the discomfort caused by the baby's pressure on my sciatic nerve. I had not looked pregnant until about the middle of the fifth month, but by the middle of the ninth I was not only large, but very stiff in places. However, I tried to do my daily dozen. On the day that the baby was due I went to the clinic, and was told all was well and the baby in a good position. I'd had a back ache the previous two nights and endless heartburn, and was very keen to be rid. On the way back to Sweet Meadow I called on a friend, who laughed at my figure and my annoyance that the newcomer had decided to be late. It was a perfect June day and I sat on the lawn and showed her how I could still touch my toes. 'For Pete's sake, stop that,' she cried. 'I don't want your infant popping out on my lawn.'

'That's a good idea,' I said, 'I'll do it again and hurry things on.' She hastily showed me to the gate.

The Pedleys were in a state of nerves at the imminence of the event. I was told to let them know when things began to happen, and Laurie would take me to the Nursing Home. As the phone was in their bedroom I was obliged to disturb them about midnight, when the backache began in real earnest. I spoke to the GP who said, 'Oh, it's a first. You'll be hours yet. Get round to the Nursing Home about breakfast time. They'll send for me if they want me.' I told the Pedleys and went back upstairs to practise my Dick Reade routine for a few hours. Janice followed me up in a terrible panic and I made her a cup of tea to steady her nerves. I knew that the frequency and strength of the pains indicated an earlier trip to the Nursing Home than the old doctor suggested, but I didn't like causing him a broken night. Between one and two o'clock in the morning it seemed best to be away with my case of necessary gear so that Janice could settle down and Laurie get back to bed and to sleep.

One poor nurse was coping with everything alone and fitted me in with her many other duties. I had hoped to have it all over before breakfast time, but the head would not crown, in spite of all my efforts. The old GP was sent for and came about eight o'clock. 'You're in a hurry,' he said. 'You've spoilt my breakfast, but at least you've not ruined my country round.' I decided there was no pleasing some people. He was impatient about the afterbirth and I had a great deal of discomfort later on – I fancy as a result of that.

However, a perfect auburn-haired eight-pound daughter was there for me to gloat over by the time he had scurried off home to finish his breakfast, take his surgery and then go off on his country round. As she lay asleep she looked a perfect picture, but she turned out to be the ace-yeller in the Nursing Home, and refused all the nurses' efforts to get her to settle to the breast. She would suck for a minute and go fast asleep. When put in with the other sleeping babies she woke up and began to raise the roof. 'You've got yourself a handful with little Copper Nob,' the nurse said prophetically.

H. had arranged to take a very short leave as soon as he had news of the baby's arrival. Janice promised to send off a telegram as soon as she knew, but her diction let me down and the station radio broadcast all day for an officer to report, whose name was unknown. It finally dawned on H. that the message might be for him, but by that time it was too late to catch a train.

I waited all day for news or the sight of him, and by night-time, after my all night vigil the previous night, I was in a very anxious state of mind. Janice had assured me she'd sent the message. My breasts were gorged and painful and we still couldn't persuade the baby to do her stuff. H. arrived late the next afternoon looking very white and shaken. He told me of the wrong name and cursed Janice's carelessness. I could see he was still terribly upset about something else. As we embraced he was ready to break down.

'What *is* the trouble?' I asked.

'Haven't they told you?' he countered incredulously.

'Told me what? Who?'

'The Pedleys. They've just told me they're selling Sweet Meadow and moving out of Beechbeck. You'll have to leave there as soon as possible. I'm still expecting an overseas posting. Where can you go? What is to become of you both?'

By the time he had gone back to his station I was in a pretty dicky state. The Nursing Home was never quiet and my room was next to the big room where the mothers seemed to thrive on endless radio and cups of strong tea. The combination reduced me to shreds. The nurses put the baby on the bottle, but she still took very little and went off to sleep until all the other babies had settled. She then let rip for all she was worth, her doll-like beauty making way for a scarlet faced virago. She was obviously fit as a fiddle, and in between her bouts would seem to mock all and sundry with a bantering, 'You'll never get me to toe the line' look. There was a tussle of wills with the Irish day nurse as well as the overworked girl on night duty. My daughter's reputation by the time we left was terrible, but they all said she was a perfect specimen physically.

Janice and Laurie drove me back to Sweet Meadow, and Janice insisted on carrying the baby indoors and was quite indignant that she should not have her way over the baby's name. Anthea and Rosalind had been two of the names on the list H. and I had considered. Left to me she would have been plain Jill, but I'd said H. should choose finally if we had a daughter. He plumped for both Anthea and Rosalind. The subtitle to the song, 'To Anthea' was – 'who may command him anything' and H. danced to his first born's tune most faithfully. I hoped that the charm of Shakespeare's Rosalind might break through the strong will eventually, and of course it did. When taken out alone by anyone she was always the most delightful and charming child, but complying with anyone else's wishes if they opposed her own was impossible.

The Pedleys were captivated by her, but we had to go ahead with plans for our departure. I had been invited to spend a fortnight with my brother Alf and his family whilst H. was trying to arrange somewhere for me to go later on. I was still very anxious and extremely tired. Anthea Rosalind thrived, but still spent hours crying. My brother thought I was too patient with her. His wife was marvellous with babies, but couldn't cope with mine.

With houses and flats almost impossible to find H. was getting desperate. His aged parents were still in poor battered London in their huge white-man's burden of a home. In the end they agreed to empty one of the bedrooms on the first floor and the big morning room behind, so that we could move all our belongings there. At least in London it would be relatively easy for H. to contact us. Travelling from the south to Beechbeck was always a very long and tedious journey.

Living with in-laws is usually fraught with difficulties. I dreaded the move from lovely old Sweet Meadow, but it had to be faced.

Laurie had objected to napkins hanging on the line and then to having them dried in the kitchen or round an old coke stove at the end of the hall. In desperation I put them on a clothes-horse round the gas fire in our sitting-room and opened the bay window to let out the steam. He said I was spoiling the paint. Janice kept popping up to tell me she was cross with him, but I found her frequent visits anything but soothing. As soon as a gas stove had been fitted into one corner of the big morning-room I moved down to London to spend an indefinite time in H.'s childhood home. The beautiful maples in the streets made a carpet for our arrival. I now did my shopping in charming old Dulwich Village and pushed out Anthea Rosalind in Dulwich Park. It was more attractive than Beechbeck with its endless winter mist, but shopping with no hope of more than rations was a very grim business.

CHAPTER TEN

LONDON AGAIN

In Beechbeck milk was plentiful and extra eggs easy to get. The butcher had always put more on the scales than anyone was really entitled to. In London it was made plain that they were doing you a favour if you got your rations. Soap flakes, which I needed for Anthea's washing, no one would part with unless they'd seen your face for years. I tramped for miles trying to get hold of some, but went back to No. 11 feeling like a criminal.

H.'s parents were thrilled because I'd been able to take a few sacks of coal down to London. They were gobbled up in no time by the rapacious old kitchen boiler, but it was hopeless trying to get enough water from the taps for washing or having a good bath. Anthea was sturdy and could push her playpen against the door if I left her whilst I tried to have a bath before the hot water was all used. On one occasion her old Grandpa offered to keep an eye on her so that I could perform my ablutions in peace. I had just stepped into the deep old bath when there was a bang, a cry of distress from Grandpa and a shriek like hell let loose from my infant. I almost wept with chagrin to leave the hot water, dry myself and struggle into my dressing gown before I'd reached for the soap. When I rushed into the morning room Grandpa was looking very upset and Anthea was purple with rage. 'I only tried to lift her up,' he explained. Poor old Grandpa. He came in every morning to see her, but had never tried to cuddle her. He was going to have a treat whilst no one was looking, but he'd no idea what a weight she was and how frail he was. He'd got her so far and she'd struggled free and fallen on the floor. Anthea was outraged that he should take such a liberty. I was very sorry for all of us – especially me, as my bath was tepid by the time I got back to it, and the boiler had had its fling for that day.

Both grandparents went down with the 'flu in the middle of the winter.

Most of the house was stone cold. They kept a coke fire burning in the dining-room and lit fires occasionally in the drawing room as long as my Beechbeck coal lasted. Their vast bedroom was like the blasted heath. I took hot drinks up to them and tried not to notice the effect of the cold on myself. Fibrositis was becoming a constant companion. To conserve fuel I lit my bedroom gas fire for Anthea's morning bath and didn't use any coke in the morning room until midday. Life was pretty grim at that time. H. was now doing a hospital job to try and polish up his medicine. Three years as senior medical officer had entailed a great deal of tiresome administration. When he came home now there were no ration cards, and I had no milk allowance for him. It meant eking out already slender resources. One day I had run up and down after the old couple and seen to the washing and shopping and was desperately hungry. My meat was gone, but I'd one egg left. I decided Anthea should have the yolk and I'd eat what she left and fill up on chips. Alas, the egg was green! In Beechbeck eggs were *never* green. I wanted to weep.

Our second year at No. 11 began, and H. applied for an 'assistantship with view' at Gravesend. That was the winter 46/47 and one of the coldest and longest in my lifetime. All the solid fuel was used up and I was reduced to queuing for emergency bags of coke and pushing them home in the pram. My stock was very low. I didn't like the name Gravesend, and I didn't fancy having to make a permanent home there. The doctor for whom H. was working had promised to try and find us a house, but he got H. settled in digs and that was that. H. was working like a nigger and his landlady could not get hold of enough food to keep him satisfied, nor fuel to keep him warm. The snow was a yard high at the sides of the roads for weeks on end. H. had kept very fit whilst he was in the Air Force, but his health declined rapidly at Gravesend. He was overworking and seeing living conditions amongst the patients which made him shudder.

He heard eventually of one house for sale, and I went over to see it. It was the end house of an old-fashioned terrace and had a huge crack from the chimneys down to the basement. I said, 'Not on your life, chum.'

After my visit to Gravesend, I was even more determined not to settle there. H. had all the rough end of the practice and absolutely no amenities in the scruffy surgery he had to use as his headquarters. I think it was our most depressing winter.

Anthea was literally all over the place. She climbed on top of the piano and broke a very pretty biscuit barrel, she winkled out my good fountain pen and threw it on the fire. I left her for a few minutes one day with the bottom of the window pushed up, and didn't realize until Spring what had happened to several favourite toys. They had finished in the big bushes outside the drawing room window below. H.'s youngest brother and his wife and baby came for Christmas. We were having pram-handle trouble and I went into Herne Hill to arrange a repair. The outing proved to be disastrous. H.'s brother asked if I'd take his watch to be repaired whilst I was down among the shops. The jeweller was closing down for alterations, so couldn't accept the watch. The garage proprietor offered to mend the pram if I went back in half an hour. I went to ring up Grandma to explain my delay and ask if she'd mind Anthea a bit longer. It began to rain and I put my handbag down in the post office to take my little umbrella out of its cover and open it. Walking out with that up and my basket on my arm I realized I'd left my handbag, but it had been snatched, and I never saw it again. All my clothing and sweet coupons, ration books, a month's money just arrived, someone else's watch and a very good handmade leather bag – all gone in no time. The police almost laughed at me and said it was happening all the time and I couldn't hope to see it again.

Anthea drank a revolting mixture of cold liver oil and orange every morning. She called it 'Oidlies,' and loved it. I had invested some of my precious coupons in Viyella and made two voluminous nightgowns for myself – hoping to keep out the cold. Alas, a sudden jerk one morning sent the oidlies down my precious nightgown. The smell remained after I'd washed it, and dear blue-eyed Florence, who came to help with the cleaning twice a week, offered to take it home. 'I was once a laundress, I can get it out for you,' she assured me. She came next time almost in tears. I didn't ask what she'd used. I viewed the wreck of my beautiful gown with dismay, but tried to comfort poor Florence. 'It's just one of those winters,' I said. 'I think the devil is in residence.' As I did my ironing next week the ironing board suddenly cracked and fell at my feet. 'Right, devil,' I said aloud, 'you're doing your damnedest, but you're not going to get *me* down.' I had a good laugh, and I'm sure he tucked his forked tail between his legs and hoofed it.

I'd had to trail over to Peckham Food Office for emergency ration cards for weeks after the handbag snatching – a very trying and depressing business, but I'd new books now and the worst of the winter was over.

H.'s six months at Gravesend were over and the doctor was very keen to sign him on for a further spell, but I was worried about his health, and begged him to try for a practice on the coast or in the country. He was accepted provisionally by a doctor on the south coast, and so left Gravesend. We waited in vain for further details from the doctor, and tried to ring him, only to discover that he'd changed his mind and gone abroad since first writing to H.

It was a blow below the belt for H. Openings in general practice were extremely difficult to get. As many as two hundred applicants were writing after each job advertised. One doctor wrote advising him to send off his applications immediately the current issue of the *British Medical Journal* was out. He, the doctor, had written to the first six of the two hundred he received. H.'s came too late, but he'd opened it as a matter of interest. 'I'm sorry, I would have preferred you,' he added to his word of advice so kindly sent. After that it became quite a desperate game. H.'s savings were dwindling and we'd nothing coming in. He was interviewed several times but I'd begged him not to take a job without definite promise of a house. One job in a very desirable group practice had a flat, but the doctor's wife there took him on one side. 'You say you have a baby? Don't risk her health here. The place is damp and rat-ridden,' she warned.

Another successful doctor said, 'Yes, you can buy my house when I've built a new one.' The said house was absolutely enormous and the entrance hall would have taken all our things comfortably. As all young doctors at that time H. would have to buy his share of the practice, and buying such a house on top of it would have left him in debt all his working life. The doctor he'd worked for at Gravesend, outwardly a very highly successful professional man, was still paying off debts to his predecessor in his fifties. H. didn't fancy the idea at all. He was offered another very tiny flat that wouldn't have taken all our modest belongings.

Weeks were passing and midsummer approaching when we saw an advertisement for a practice in north Wales. 'Good house empty, beautiful district. Terms to be agreed mutually.' It was a locum with a view to partnership they wanted, and my husband was invited to take us along for a holiday and stay in the doctor's house whilst he took a long holiday in Scotland. The maid would be there and a relation who did the dispensing. A heaven-spent opportunity!

H. decided he would have to have his own car for the job, and cast around to buy one. By this time anything on wheels was being snatched up and ridiculous prices asked for vehicles which were little better than heaps of scrap metal. He went forth one day with our pooled resources in his pocket and returned with Horace. It was a prehistoric Ford with TROUBLE written large all over it. I hated it on sight.

However, we were facing our first long spell in the country since leaving Beechbeck, and I was longing to see H. putting away some eggs and good food again. As we piled our belongings into Horace I thought of the empty house at the other end and my spirits rose.

H. had not done much driving since passing through the hands of his instructor, and he was extremely jumpy. Not that Horace was designed to inspire confidence. The wonder was that he went at all. Once we'd left London behind and got on to the marvellous old Roman road to Wales we found very little traffic and we began to enjoy the journey. As a child I'd been a shocking car traveller, but I decided the jolty old car was perhaps good for travel sickness, or else having a baby had changed my chemistry for the better.

But for a little girl of almost two it was a very long day. She kept asking where we were going. 'To Doctor Farnell's,' I answered. 'Are we nearly at Docti Fa's?' she asked then. At about four o'clock we stopped for tea, and to give H. a break. Anthea had some food and trotted about a bit to stretch her legs. We got back on to the road and began the last two hours' journey. No sooner had we begun than Anthea turned green and was very sick. After that we had many stops and many moppings up. We finally drove up the long drive to Dr Farnell's house with Anthea saying with great relief

'It's Docti Fa's.' Poor old Horace had made it. We left the reeking car and staggered wearily to the door of the old house.

Dr Farnell welcomed us very warmly. He was a small slightly-built man, with white hair, rosy cheeks and great personal charm. His wife seemed somewhat younger and the presence of their adorable seven-year-old daughter suggested that she was at least fifteen years younger than her husband. It was very much a home that had seen the wear and tear of a family, in spite of some very beautiful antique furniture here and there. In addition to the doctor, his wife and daughter and the youngest of their three sons there was a resident maid and an elderly aunt living in the house. A full time gardener – an old man – and a part time younger one were also attached to the household.

The elderly aunt – a trained nurse (trained when nurses had £12 per year and worked endless hours) had been persuaded to leave Italy, which she loved, to come and nurse the second son of the family. He had subsequently died of meningitis. The first son, a lively attractive boy, had also died during the war. The parents were absolutely stricken by the deaths of the two sons in quick succession. The third son had obviously been very badly shaken by the loss of his two elder brothers. The little girl had been an unwanted 'runner-up' in the family, but the aunt insisted that she had saved the sanity of her parents when they were facing their terrible loss. That she was spoilt goes without saying. The remaining son seemed like a ship without a rudder, poor lad.

The house stood on a steep hillside and the drive went round a tiny copse up to a terrace in front of the main door. At the edge of the terrace was an enormous weeping ash, which gave a welcome shade on very hot days. Here the aunt fed the birds and swore at the cat in Italian when he tried to catch the birds. She stayed with us to act as dispenser and to take care of the lamps. Yes, it was the only house in the village without electricity. Originally it had been the first to have electricity, as the previous owner – a very brisk and businesslike man – had installed his own donkey engine.

When the village was finally provided with an electricity supply by an enterprising Mr Smith, the doctor's house was linked by a cable through the little copse.

Alas, Dr Farnell's three boys were also enterprising, and fitted up fairy lights amongst the trees, and I believe amongst more trees in a little screen behind the house. Smith the Light found this an unfair drain on his resources. As it was, the street lights were very dim when the weekly cinema show was on, and it was said that ironing day caused a bit of anxiety. The doctor's sons were warned, but took no heed. Smith the Light then took the law into his own hands and cut the cable. Thus it came about that the electric light flexes were tied up in squiggles for the spiders to play in, and Aunt Agnes spent a lot of time seeing to lamps and placing them at strategic places throughout the big old house.

In the kitchen was an extremely old coal range. It had a hole in the side of the oven, and after the first flush of activity in the early morning it sulked. Rice puddings it managed – with more eggs in one than our joint week's ration in London – but roasting meat was not 'on'. It so came about that the beautiful succulent joints of beef brought to the house were cut in two and cooked in a large iron saucepan on the fire. It was a very novel way of cooking a joint, but it worked. One half was always kept for Monday, as the maid's mother came then to battle with the large wash in the wash-house across the yard. It was the thing to see that she was well-fed in the middle of her arduous task.

You may wonder where the money came for the pay and support of so many people. So did we, for it was understood that we would move into the big house and reign supreme in a few years' time, if we found we got on well in the practice. Dr Farnell was not a business man. The income for the whole practice was less than H. had been offered to stay on at Gravesend. It explained the shabbiness of all the furnishings and the fact that Mrs Farnell was trying to add to the income by writing for magazines. The doctor had tried unsuccessfully to run a garage, we were told. The young son had a van and a beautiful roadster, and his father two small cars and one big family car kept for holidays. Poor Horace looked very humble fry amongst such company, and H. was invited to use one of the small cars for the practice.

When the family left for Scotland I was officially in charge of the housekeeping, and wept to see so much fruit dropping off bushes and beautiful vegetables spoilt by the maid's bad cooking. I took that over and gathered and bottled the blackcurrants and gooseberries. I made the strawberries and raspberries into jam, as far as the sugar would allow, and left the larder shelves looking quite well-stocked.

H. drove off to the tiny village surgeries – often a chair in someone's front room, with the patients waiting outside in the street. The truth was there were very few patients – either at the main surgery or in the villages. If he saw six or seven patients he'd had a busy day. There was time to lie in the sun in the little meadow where the washing was pegged out, and time to go and investigate the mysteries of Smith The Light's contrivances. Anthea had the loan of the toys of the household and these included a tiny battered perambulator with a large hole in the hood. She always insisted on having the hood up, and then rammed the dolls in so that their heads shot out of the hole behind. She strutted down the village street in front of me announcing to all and sundry that she had the dollies in a 'PARM'.

Curtains moved and faces peeped round to watch us. There was a real Dylan Thomas atmosphere. In the village where the empty house 'for us' was, the people rarely spoke English. Behind the house was an enormous slag heap. The house was indeed spacious enough and the garden full of fruit trees. After our protracted search for a job with a definite house it seemed terrible to be at all critical, but the different language, the moving curtains, the slag heap and above all the lack of work and adequate income drove us to careful scrutiny of the columns in the B.M.J. again.

We heard from Scotland that the family would like us to stay longer than the pre-arranged time, and we accepted gratefully, for the good food, rest and fresh air had been a Godsend after our difficult winter, but we knew we couldn't settle there permanently.

On one outing in the village I was met by an elderly lady coming out of a cottage. She was very friendly and said, 'Your husband is the locum, isn't he?' I said that it was so. 'I used to live where you are staying,' she went on, 'I was the previous doctor's second wife!' She asked if we would take coffee with her one day, and we were pleased to go.

What an interesting tale she told over the coffee and biscuits. As a young woman she had been a teacher in the next village, travelling backwards and forwards in her own little pony trap. Very tragically her sister and her brother-in-law died leaving four children. She took them into her own little home and cared for them as well as possible on her small income. It was her habit to leave the pony at home on Friday so that her nieces and nephews could ride him on Saturdays – she thought he had more energy to be worked off if he'd rested all day on Friday. It meant a fairly long walk for her, and one Friday she was overtaken by the doctor in his gig. He asked what was wrong with her pony, and offered her a lift. She explained that she tried to spoil the orphaned children a bit. The doctor was a widower with three children. The eventual outcome of the first lift was his proposal. 'You've got four fatherless children in that tiny house and I've got three motherless ones in my big house, the sensible thing would be to join forces. Could you face bringing up seven children – none of them yours?' She decided to accept the challenge.

In those days the doctor's house was kept spick and span, and it was the only one boasting electricity. The doctor was a very kind man but very particular. As he grew older one of his locums married his daughter and settled in the district as an assistant. He was bored. It was not a busy practice. One way of beating boredom was to leave the village by car when the train left the station and try and get to the next village – tearing along the narrow high-hedged roads, before the train reached the next station. There was one ungated level-crossing to negotiate first. There came the dreadful day when the little train and the dashing car met at the level crossing.

The old doctor died, his children and the other four were gone and the practice and house were sold. The poor old house was certainly past its heyday, but a beautiful curved staircase leading up from the hall hinted at its former glory.

The water pipes were always leaking, inside and out. Jones the Fish, a gentleman of parts, was part-time village plumber. He was 'open' for fish in his front room about twice a week. I think his throat was open to ale almost anytime, and if you could catch him at home he made promises and eventually came with his bag of tricks to cope with the latest leak. As often as not his hammerings and screwings seemed to set off another leak, and a modest river followed him down the drive as his beacon of a nose led the way to his next job.

At the end of six weeks we were becoming as lazy and relaxed as the air, but it was incumbent upon us to stir old Horace into activity on H.'s day off and to go and look at a practice in Derbyshire. Horace had behaved very badly on his few airings in Wales. The stronger air on the Pennines upset him completely. We arrived at the appointment very late and careworn. The doctor's wife met us – a large, very gracious lady – and was most sympathetic about Horace. She took to Anthea and I thought things seemed promising. However, her husband did not like to be kept waiting. He'd been running a very busy two-man practice single-handed during the war. His wife, a nurse, had obviously been working like a Trojan to give him every possible support, but he was tired out. After battling his way there in Horace my husband was far from his most serene. We looked at the flat prepared for the future assistant. It was the second floor of the doctor's large Elizabethan house, but the windows were small and gave little light. The doctor's wife and I got on like a house on fire, but the doctor parted with us with all his guards up, saying he'd several more to see and he'd let us know.

Unfortunately Horace refused to go home to Wales. We struggled in vain, and in the end had to ask the doctor to help us get him to the top of the hill, in the hope that the engine would spark off when we coasted down the other side. His expression had not been at all 'come hither' before. My last glance at his face, as Horace grudgingly came to life, made me say to H., 'Well, that's the last we'll see of this nice place.' It was!

The Farnells came back from Scotland, paid H. handsomely for what had been virtually a much-needed holiday, and said they were very sorry we weren't staying on. We thanked them for their kindness, they thanked me for the jam and preserved fruit on the shelves and we went back much fitter to London. H. had sent applications all over the country whilst we were still in Wales, and we were anxious to collect our post.

When we went together to look at practices I was struck by the careworn faces of most of the doctors' wives. Large houses inadequately staffed, patients invading the family quarters twice a day, palatial fronts and very seedy backs – my eyes began to open and I wondered just what I'd let myself in for. There was an opportunity to join a London practice and with

125

it a flat – groundfloor, very pokey and very dark. The doctor was leaving to go overseas. One of his three children had pernicious anaemia. He was a frail little fellow lying in bed when we looked over the flat. It was a terribly depressing place, and again the wife looked stretched to the limit.

Before I married, my dentist had teased me and said that doctors' wives spent all their time at bridge parties. From remarks dropped out to me it seemed they spent their lives answering phones, cleaning surgeries and trying to care for their families and keep their chins up against great odds. One beautiful Canadian woman in a fashionable spa told me the house was really dropping to pieces, and she found the formal social life of the town a great bind. Twice a day patients walked through the middle of her home along the hall with rotting floor boards underneath. The senior partner's wife there sat in an enormous room, which I admired. She said that everyone loved the house excepting herself. She couldn't get reliable help and answering the phone and keeping the huge old house clean wore her to a shadow. Her husband was a cocky little fellow, and the mansion was obviously a status symbol as far as he was concerned. No daily help would stay and cope with the endless cleaning.

There was a practice on the East coast which was very desirable, but no house was available. The doctor there said he'd try to locate a house. Then we heard of one on the outskirts of a Northern city with a house available in November. I knew the city slightly – a vigorous, go-ahead university town. H. travelled alone to see the place. He came back quite excited. 'There's a Methodist Church next door but one, and a branch of your bank opposite and a beautiful library within a stone's throw. They really are moving out in November and will put me up from the first of September.' The reference to my bank must be explained. My banking had begun as a child in The Yorkshire Penny Bank, which H. had never heard of. When he saw the name he was sure that we would be settling in Cockburn.

He wrote and accepted the offer of assistantship with view to partnership six months later.

Within the week we heard from the East coast practice that the doctor had found a house and we were also accepted somewhere else. After so long everything came at once, but we'd plumped for Cockburn.

CHAPTER ELEVEN

COCKBURN

I was invited to take Anthea up there for a fortnight whilst the doctor and his wife were on holiday. On their return I travelled back to London and H. stayed on as assistant until the doctor and his family moved further out into the country. There was another assistant of long standing, and he and the senior were both short and stocky. When H. stood between them they made a most comical trio. The senior was always in a hurry and 'on the make', and the other was incredibly slow and always down to twopence. He was very sympathetic, and the patients loved him. When he came in they felt no one else in the world mattered. If he ran late, which he nearly always did, they were quite reconciled to being knocked up by him at eleven at night. His wife never knew when he was coming home for a meal. He had a camel-like capacity for eating enough at one sitting to last for hours and hours.

My skinny spouse had to be fed bang on meal times or his temper became very frayed. It was just painful to wait for two minutes longer.

Swiss Cottage was one of the big houses built when Cockburn first became a dormitory site for the big industrial city. It had a very large pleasant lounge, a north-facing room which we furnished as a study, and a very large kitchen. Beyond the kitchen were small outhouses which had been converted as surgery and waiting room. The old scullery was the dispensary. There were six bedrooms and a box room, bathroom and so on.

The senior's wife, a very shy and extremely kind and generous woman, was a keen gardener. The front garden was well stocked and a small fairly secluded garden beyond the garage had a little pond, a big rockery, strawberry bed, apple tree and a few conifers. In one corner was a Heath Robinson summer house.

It was the end of November before the house was vacant, and I travelled through sleet and rain to find H. and a kindly niece still trying to clean up the house and settle in our furniture. The latter had been taken up overnight, and as the senior doctor and his wife had crowded two households of furniture into Swiss Cottage their removal men were still struggling to empty the place when ours arrived. Years of accumulated dust and fluff from behind furniture bowled down the stairs. My gallant niece stayed for a week or two and we gradually got the ground floor and first floor ship-shape. In one of the attic rooms the senior had left an old battered desk absolutely choc-a-bloc with forms and rubbish of every description. The paper hung off damp walls up there, and we discovered later the rain ran down one chimney and across the floor.

The big sunny lounge took our dining and three-piece suites, the piano, an oak chest and was still spacious. The outbuildings took up the light from the kitchen window, and the dust from the unmade side-road joined the still-swirling leaves and made a messy heap outside the dispensary door. As often as not the senior and the older assistant left this door open and the North wind swept under our kitchen door and made the house terribly cold. In the evenings it was still the same, and often the two trotted through to the hall to see if I'd taken any late messages and then went out leaving all the doors open. We felt the sudden drop in temperature even two yards from the lounge fire, and I was profoundly thankful when we could lock the doors about eleven o'clock and feel we had the place to ourselves. The mud gathered by their shoes was often scraped off on the lower shelf of the telephone table, but I cleaned up after them and counted my blessings.

It was soon obvious that our kitchen was really the social hub of the practice. In the coldest weather I bought bones and made pints of good broth, and at other times gallons of coffee for all and sundry. Special patients for injections, private patients or the vicar, were told to wait in my kitchen. If the senior's wife came into Cockburn to shop and needed a lift home she called. The doctors stopped for a drink in the middle of hectic surgeries or in the middle of big visiting sessions. From there I dashed to answer the phone in the hall or to answer the knocks or rings on the dispensary door. All practice news and shop tended to be passed on over a 'cuppa'.

In the middle of all this I coped with my washing, ironing, cooking and so on. It was a hectic life, but I was thankful to be living a useful life and not to feel like a soul in limbo, as I had seemed in my two years in London. I had made friends there, but they all had their husbands at home and I felt that our life together was being shelved indefinitely.

My eldest niece, Mary, suffered from asthma, and her school career had been badly affected. I knew she was not trained for any career and was at a loose end. As Muriel, the niece who had helped over the move was now beginning her training as a nurse, I wrote to Mary and asked if she would like to come to Cockburn and help me until she saw another more desirable job. She was fond of children and able to take Anthea out. She had a very clear voice and coped with the phone well. The patients and the doctors and old book-keeper took to her. Her health improved by leaps and bounds and she had soon put on a stone in weight and grown into an attractive young woman. I took her round to join the Youth Club at the Methodist Church and she made congenial friends of her own age for the first time.

Settled at last, we decided to have another child. By the following summer I was smitten with my old enemy phlebitis. One of Mary's duties was to see to the lounge fire and to answer the phone when I was resting in the afternoon. But Mary loved the garden, and the phone could not be heard from the little garden beyond the garage. One afternoon the phone went and I realized Mary must be outside. I got up and decided to rest on the settee in case it went again. It was chilly in the big lounge and Mary had forgotten about the fire. I went down into the cellar – a very damp one – and chopped sticks. In the middle of my activity Mary called down from the hall, 'Aunt Nancy, where is the little spade?' I told her, and tried not to show my annoyance at her desertion of her post when I was supposed to be resting. I went up the cellar steps with my sticks and some coal and found she had shot the bolt on the door from the hall. I called in vain for some time, and then went to the coal chute, which was fairly near the dispensary door, hoping I could make her hear from there. Not a hope! I shouted myself hoarse, and knowing that there was no one to answer the phone unless I surfaced I climbed on top of the coal, struggled with the heavy iron grating covering the chute, and finally emerged – filthy and extremely angry.

Some time later Mary said, 'You know I only ever saw you really angry once, Aunty.' She didn't need to say when. I'm afraid asthmatics tend to be dreamers, and yet are often so lovable.

She was blessed with a very good ear and a tuneful voice. Her parents were both good singers. An aunt on her mother's side was keen that she should have violin lessons now that she was living on the outskirts of a city. We found a teacher with a good reputation and she began lessons. He was pleased to have a pupil with a natural aptitude and said she was able to do things instinctively that others tried in vain to do. As she never touched the violin excepting on the day of her lesson, when she had a quick bash before catching the bus, it staggered me that she progressed at all. In retrospect I can see that she was not all that much naughtier than I had been myself over my piano lessons.

I was concerned that she should train for some sort of career, and discussed her with our minister. He was a very human and sagacious man, and suggested that she might train as a sister in the National Children's Homes. A compulsory English and Arithmetic paper must be written and then it was a case of general aptitude and personality. He wrote to the principal of the training school in London and told them about her indifferent health record, adding quite truthfully that she seemed to be leaving the weakness behind. They accepted her application and it was arranged for her to begin a pre-College year at their attractive branch at Harrogate.

However, before she left us our son was born. Three days before he was due we went to visit Doug who was living about fourteen miles north of York. We had planned to go blackberrying, as Doug always knew where to find plenty. My phlebitis had settled and I was quite active, climbing up steep banks, stretching here and bending there. Going home in the car I had a nasty backache. When H. and Mary sat around waiting for me to give them their supper I felt very jaded and a bit peeved.

I tried to settle in bed and found the backache much worse. About two o'clock I decided it was more than backache and told H. I was going into the little bedroom I'd prepared for the event. He decided not to wake Mary, but to warn the sister we'd booked to come and attend the delivery. He then went into the kitchen to persuade the stove to light and provide plenty of hot water. I tried to tell him not to bother, but the contractions were too strong and I couldn't speak. And so, as often happens with a second baby, our son waited on no ceremony and was born with no one in attendance at all. I heard later that Dr Pease's son, also a second child, had arrived under exactly similar circumstances in the same room eighteen years earlier.

It was a pleasant little room facing east, with a mountain ash tree outside the window. Christopher was a very loving and contented child from the moment he saw daylight.

It was a very foggy morning and H. went off with cards and notes to relations, with Anthea skipping along beside him carolling, 'It's a misty, moisty morning and I've got a baby brother.'

He was a few weeks old when Mary left us to go to Harrogate.

The following weeks must have been the most hectic of my life. We advertised and got a daily help who worked at the double and hated Mondays and broke something regularly. She had worked for a doctor before and her previous mistress had been a semi-invalid. Because of that she was used to doing absolutely everything. I told her there was no need for such a rush. Of course when she was not there I had the phone and the door to answer no matter what I was trying to do for my family. Sometimes I had to answer the phone whilst I had the baby on the pot. He had to be tucked under one arm, pot and all, whilst I answered the phone in my best professional manner and wrote the message with my free hand. Sometimes I left him sitting in the bath, scared stiff he would fall on his face before I got back. At the busiest time of year – usually January to March – we could have as many as twelve calls during breakfast.

But the worst torture of all was the night bell. It was situated under our bedroom window about a yard from the bed. The noise it made was indescribably soul-destroying. There had been a similar one in the bedroom we occupied in Wales, and although we'd had little work there we had had a few night calls. People panic in the small hours. Crises which at nine-thirty in the evening seem bearable become unbearable at about two in the morning. After the wretched bell had gone my whole system seemed keyed up waiting for it to go again.

At that time H. could turn out of bed, cope with the situation, and then go to sleep again. I'm afraid he has become more like me now, and contrariwise I am much more capable of pushing my good ear into the pillow and going to sleep again. In fact one night he was called out of bed three times, and that particular week he was called out eight times in five nights. It was wearying to a degree, but we were living at the main practice house and that was where most of the calls were taken.

At weekends, before the Health Service began, patients used to call on their way to the shops to pay off something on their bills. It is hard to believe now, but they would often come with a pound note and ask to pay off a shilling. If H. decided to do some gardening on his half-day the same thing would happen, or they would decide to have a little consultation out of normal surgery hours. Unless we got right away there was no peace.

Once the Health Service had begun there were all the record cards to be made up, and H. used to make quick notes on slips of paper and then spend ages every night writing the notes on to the cards. It was obvious that we were in desperate need of more practice accommodation and a secretary. Dr Pease had promised that all the ground floor of Swiss Cottage would be converted into spacious consulting and waiting rooms, and that the two upper floors would be made into a convenient maisonette for our family use. Of course nothing came of these promises. He hated parting with money and we must cope the best we could. Mrs Yorke, the older assistant's wife, had warned me what the situation would be like, but H. like most people had been taken in by Dr Pease's jovial manner and lavish promises. We were at first willing slaves, but soon became so exhausted that we knew we would have to make a break.

We wrote to an organisation which arranged for foreign women to come as resident maids. H decorated the smallest bedroom at the top of the house and we bought some furniture. Unfortunately there was a white slave scare at that time and the French girl we were expecting never turned up. The next one was a German woman. She was supposed to be able to answer the telephone and speak fluent English. We sent the money for her fare and the substantial fee to the agency, having been assured that she had no ties in Germany and would be able to stay with us indefinitely. What a hope!

H. went to meet her boat at Hull. He rang me latish that evening to say that the crossing was extremely bad and the boat was not expected until morning. He had to spend the night there. He sprained his foot that night and when he turned up next day his ankle was very swollen and painful. The German maid was still looking green after her difficult crossing and she could not speak three clear words of English. I showed her up to her room and hoped that my scanty German would mean something to her. She seemed very frightened, as if expecting us to be harsh with her.

However, she was a willing worker and took to Anthea immediately. She played 'rough House' games with her and chatted to her in German. It was obvious that she could not answer the phone, and I had to arrange for someone else to be in when we went off for a few hours on H.'s half day. We left her in charge of the children, and the lady who came to scrub the surgery in charge of the phone one day, but when we returned Anthea was waiting for us white-faced and frightened, and Christopher had a burn across his hand where he had crawled to the electric fire unnoticed by the maid. I dared not leave her alone with them again.

She picked up a bit of English and with my scanty German we managed to communicate. For a time she settled and began to attend a multi-racial club in the city on her day off, and to go into the big library there. One day she returned in a great state and told me that a man in the library had spat at her and called her a dirty German pig. It sounded most un-English to me. She had lied about her commitments in Germany and was sending money to Hamburg regularly. Her husband was still a prisoner in Russian hands and it was suddenly announced that they were releasing the last of them. After that Charlotte watched every post for a letter and got more and more sullen as one didn't come. In the end one did and she seemed almost distracted. The following day off she left the house in a black mood and did not return in the evening.

Late that night we still had no news of her, and I wondered what sinister things were going on in the city. In the end we rang the police, who took the attitude that it was not in the least surprising. They advised us to put her in a taxi with her belongings and tell her to 'Git!' when she turned up. I said we were responsible for her, but they seemed to think I was barmy.

The next morning she turned up exhausted and said she'd been to Hull to find out about boats. The letter was from her husband who said she must go back at once or he'd get another woman. She assured me that I couldn't understand what German women put up with, as I had a good husband. Her husband's health was broken and he would take another woman into the flat she'd been sending rent for. She said I'd been very kind to her and she'd come back and work for me and pay off all she owed us later on, but she must go back now. Her baby had been killed in an air-raid.

So H. had to drive the poor soul back to Hull and pay her fare. It had been a costly experience in every way, and I tried to get daily help from the Labour Exchange after that. One they sent was mentally deficient, another turned up dressed to the nines to be interviewed and then arrived to start work with dirty bare feet in old sandals, and reeking, once she'd removed her outer garments. She'd obviously never cleaned herself, let alone a room. She admitted that she lived in one room with her fifteen-year-old son. I wept when she'd gone, and decided to keep her if she'd take a bath and wear some of my clothes whilst I cleaned hers. But she didn't turn up a second time.

My third effort from the Exchange had five children and a drunken husband. The latter was a miner when he worked, but an expert at having accidents. When he got his compensation he went off to Doncaster, Wetherby or York to the races. When he was broke he came home again. There were continual anxieties over whether the furniture would be taken away because the instalments were not paid. She was a puny, wretched little woman, but an expert at cleaning brass. Amos, our old grandfather clock, always shone in her short reign, as did the brass door knobs and light switches. The children she left behind got into trouble with the police, and the little ones were sick. In the end she vanished with one of my good overalls. I'd given her clothes for the children, but our own resources were very slender at the time. I posted on the money we owed her and carried on for six weeks with no help at all. The old book-keeper was greatly relieved when she went. He had been fond of Mary and found anyone else very trying. He was outraged when the mother of five brought all the gang and their washing along when we were on holiday. She washed their dirty clothes along with some very good clothes belonging to Christopher. I had not

Anthea and Chris.

asked her to do any washing, as I preferred to do that myself. I'd had things ruined so often if I let them out of my own hands. It happened again. Beautiful white hand-knitted clothes had been reduced to grey, and put in hot water into the bargain. They were hard and not fit to use. I, too, was relieved at her departure, but I knew that as the practice work increased in the winter I would have to try to get someone else. I didn't relish trying again, but one day a small bright-eyed young woman turned up at the door. 'I've been told you are looking for help. If you're not fixed up I'd like to come.' It was Joan – heaven sent – young, clean, eager to please and pleasant with everyone. She was a great help for a long time, but subsequently left the district. Last year she turned up to visit us and said the things I'd taught her had been the most valuable she'd ever learned. I can't think what things she meant, but it was nice of her to say it.

After her departure – much regretted on both sides – we were blessed with a slap-happy lady who propped herself on the nearest bit of furniture and watched whatever I was doing. 'Oh, that's how you do that. I've often wondered,' she usually said afterwards. When I turned my back she apparently did nothing at all, but she turned up regularly and I was able to go out to the shops with an easy conscience. If I left the phone in the hands of the book-keeper he was apt to pick it up when it rang and then slam it down without answering. He loathed the thing.

A relation several times removed rang me up one day. 'I've just heard of a very capable housekeeper, Nancy. She knows your area and would be just the person for you. I told her you were desperate and she says she can start at once.'

I demurred, as I felt I was being bulldozed. 'But I've got a daily help now.'

'You don't mean that idle woman I saw the other week, do you? I'm talking about an experienced residential housekeeper – used to coping with everything. I told her you'd be sure to want her.'

I felt very uneasy, having been bitten so often, but I agreed to interview the lady. It was my undoing. She was twenty years older than I and used to having her own way. I said I couldn't dismiss Mrs Propper immediately and was told they could work together for a few days. I knew good-natured old Propper was thoroughly idle, but I didn't like the look in the eye of Miss Ouster. After two days in her company Propper said she'd go. She added that she wasn't used to being treated like dirt by a woman like that Miss Ouster.

No sooner had she gone than Miss Ouster said she must have a 'Friday woman' to do the heavy cleaning. She offered to pay her out of her own money and to get one from an agency she used herself. At any rate the 'Friday woman' was a great treasure – clean, reliable, cheerful, generous-hearted, she saw me through many a difficult time.

Miss Ouster began to ogle the two older doctors and to knock against them accidentally when they passed through the kitchen to look at the message book. She poured all the cream off the milk (and at that time I took a gallon very often) and drank it when no one was looking. If I made any suggestions she flew into a paddy. I found her presence odious, but I daren't sack her.

In the end I rang up the distant relation and asked just what she knew about the woman. It all came out then. Since she'd contacted me she had learnt from the friend who had previously housed Miss Ouster that she was a thoroughly bad lot. The cream-drinking was one of her special lines, but there were others, and the friend had been absolutely at her wits' end when she asked my relation if she knew of anyone who wanted a housekeeper. I was pretty hopping mad. H. gave her notice, and she said she'd take her 'Friday woman' when she went, but the said 'Friday woman' was very happy with us, and agreed to stay on and bring a friend to help on days when she couldn't come. Miss Ouster had done us one good turn.

All unwittingly she did us another. She had stayed in very short skirts when everyone else was 'new-looking' and in addition she wore low-necked blouses. Every morning as she polished the brasses on the front door she stood with the door ajar in a very strong draught. She took a shocking cold and soaked innumerable hankies. To my horror she dried them out over the kitchen stove, without washing and disinfecting them. I tried to stop it, but she shouted me down – saying they were only wet. As a result the kitchen was full of germs and Christopher and H. went down with very bad infections. They were both extremely ill. Anthea and I took it, but just kept on our feet. Dr Pease went up to see H. and hinted that he'd got T.B.

Overworking ever since he'd arrived, it needed only that to send H. to the depths of despair. I said we'd get out of the practice house if it was the last thing we did. Miss Ouster insisted in having a local paper. We never had time to read newspapers, but I took one for her. Whilst H. was in bed I searched the columns for a house in the area. I saw one near the park in a pleasant, quiet road and went to look over it. I had always sworn I'd have no more to do with big houses with attics and cellars, but I forgot when I went through the gates. There was a huge garden with apple trees laden with blossom, and two lawns, the lower one the size of a tennis court. The house had a happy atmosphere and seemed a reasonable price. I got in a member of the Methodist Church who dealt in property and asked him to vet the place. He said it was a good buy, and advised H. to buy it through an insurance. Poor H. signed all the papers without even seeing the place. I was determined to get out of Dr Pease's clutches and to have a home with some privacy. I knew we'd have to face a shindy and not be able to move until someone had been found to live at the surgery, but H. was an equal partner by now and I felt should not have all the donkey work to do and all the night calls.

In the end it worked out the practice house was made into a flat and a maisonette – still none of the modern premises we'd been promised for the surgery. Dr Pease's old maid was offered the flat in exchange for duties as a part-time telephonist and receptionist, and at long last an older woman was installed as secretary-receptionist for surgeries. It was a great feat.

I still had the phone linked with mine, and did a lot of extra duties in that line, but for the first time since arriving in Cockburn I could take the children into the park and sit in my own garden in privacy. It took months to adapt to doing either without worrying about the telephone and so on. I had not realized just how drained I was by the four years at Swiss Cottage. Another doctor and his wife in the area had had a very similar experience, and his health was almost broken by the time they moved out of the practice house. His wife was as tired as I was, and they moved several miles out into the country. We were only one third of a mile from the surgery house, but it was like a different world. We had no night bell as such, and the old regulars who used to seek us out at all times of day and night never located us. Calls taken at the surgery were passed on to the doctor concerned, generally, and although H. took rather more than his share he could stretch out on the lawn on his day off if he wanted to, and stare at the sky and relax.

We had been married just ten years when we finally moved into our own home – Copperfield, Pemberton Green.

CHAPTER TWELVE

PEMBERTON GREEN

I did not regret the years at Swiss Cottage. In many ways a doctor's wife has a worm's eye view of the community, but one learns a great deal about people. I remembered how jumpy the senior partner had been when an old soul had a heart attack and died in the surgery. He had called me through from the kitchen, and I stood and held her hand until the ambulance came. He thanked me gratefully. I was pregnant at the time and he seemed surprised that I was not scared to be with the poor tired old body. On another occasion two sisters came round, middle-aged women. One had a shocking nose bleed. It was out of surgery hours and I did what I could. They finally went and I washed the blood from the floor. I felt a bit queasy at the end of the exercise and went outside to have a breather in the little herb garden I'd grown near the dispensary. To my disgust I found the two ladies had left me a present of a blood-soaked handkerchief in the drain outside the kitchen window. I picked it up and disposed of it, and gave free rein to my feelings about people who seem to be decent types and do a trick like that. Next morning a beautiful bunch of flowers arrived for me with a note from the two ladies thanking me for all my kindness. I felt very small. By the time I left I could recognise hundreds of voices on the phone when about three words had been spoken, but it was not until we moved to Pemberton Green that I became anyone's neighbour in any real sense of the word. 'Popping in' anywhere had been out of the question.

Now I could saunter back from the shops and talk to my neighbours. Pemberton Green was mainly houses built immediately before the First World War. No two pairs were exactly alike, and the builder had designed Copperfield for himself. It was the last of the houses built at that time, and he had kept the next double plot for his side garden. The dining room faced this and gave a lovely view of the lawns, apple trees and borders. Unfortunately the people who had occupied the house for eighteen months before we took over had done absolutely nothing in the garden, and it was almost impossible to tell where the lawns ended and the borders began.

We borrowed a scythe for the lawns and pulled nettles a yard high from amongst the roses. As we had to wait until August before moving in we went round on our half-days and tackled the garden. I had seen over the house in May after a long dry spell. Decorators had just whitewashed the cellars. I asked about damp and was told there was none. Alas, the weather broke just after we'd bought the house, and before we moved in large green patches showed through the whitewash in the cellar and an immense patch of black mould appeared on the newly-papered wall of the lounge. Rain poured from a broken gutter over the dining-room bay and formed a pool on the floor inside. We were shattered, but couldn't help loving the old house. There had been a very happy family in the place for nineteen years before the neglectful people we'd bought it from. They had kept the garden like a park, we were told, but had apparently not seen to the fabric of the house. We could see it needed a new garage and gate and the drive re-surfaced, but the damp had not shown because of the dry winter.

However, we knew the price had not been high and we felt we couldn't complain – even when we found dry rot in the window ledges and skirtings of our bedroom. We began a campaign which went on for a long time until we'd got everything sound, and modernized the kitchen as a final grand gesture. We were never sorry we'd bought the place. The views were good from all the windows and we had most pleasant and kindly neighbours. We felt we'd come home at last. In our ten years of married life we'd lived in eight places and were very reluctant to look on a removal van again.

We decided to celebrate and have another baby, and the July after we moved into Copperfield the pram was out beneath the beautiful willow tree at one corner of the lawn. I'd had a roughish time whilst carrying her, and phlebitis attacked immediately after her birth, but we were delighted to welcome Julia Nan, even if she was a bit over-cooked and bore a remarkable resemblance to a tar-brush crossed with a beetroot. Like her seven year old sister she had a fine pair of lungs, which she exercised religiously every

Baby Julia.

evening from about six thirty to ten o'clock. Having done her duty she usually took her feed with the air of someone who'd earned it, and slept through the night. She often gave tongue in the garden in the morning and could be heard at the end of the road. She had a dark enquiring eye and never missed a thing. From an early age she became a wig and would stand on the arms of her high chair and shriek for very joy. Christopher would almost roll with laughing. He appreciated all her antics and absolutely adored her. She was not a beauty for a year or two. Her bonnets always fell over her eyes and clothes never looked right on her until she was over two. H. called her 'Bad but beautiful', and she was very proud of her title, and most resourceful in finding out little wickednesses to justify her name.

As Julia was born in midsummer we decided to have a holiday at West Burton in September. It was extremely bleak and wintry weather, and Christopher, recovering from a tonsillectomy, developed bronchitis and had an attack of asthma. The specialist had delayed his operation, hoping that his condition would improve, but had reluctantly decided to remove the enlarged tonsils and adenoids in the end. Christopher had been stricken with eczema since the age of two and was a likely subject for asthma, but his mouth-breathing had become very bad and his general health had been getting worse for some time.

It was the beginning of years of trouble compared with which the eczema was of little consequence. He was extremely patient and brave over his repeated attacks and rarely, if ever, called out for help. Perhaps he couldn't. I heard him through the bedroom wall and went to do what I could and to stay with him until the attacks subsided. He became a great reader, especially of animal books and could quote facts and figures relating to animals of all shapes and sizes. Sometimes he drew funny little pictures. One memorable one was of a dog boy scout making toast at a camp fire.

When he was in the nursing home for his operation his character changed. H. had taken his boon companion, a large Teddy bear, and he blamed him for all that went wrong. 'Ted kept ringing for the nurse when he didn't want her. Ted wouldn't eat his dinner. Ted was an awful nuisance in the nursing home.' The nurses were jolly glad to see the back of Ted, and we were staggered to hear of the reputation he'd built up for his normally very considerate master!

On his return home tales of Ted became part of our daily life. We had a new chapter related every day, and wonderful creatures were added to the characters in the plot. There was the dauntless duck whose name was Snake-pecker, and so on. He occasionally drew little figures, but he showed no leaning towards writing. Anthea could pick out letters at three and was reading quite well before she began school. Julia was the same. Chris could talk very fluently and had a marvellous vocabulary, but he had to learn to spell his name by learning a tune to it. That worked very well. The prospect of school held no lure for him. He loved his home and the garden, the cat and the hedgehog, but, along with another doctor's son and a later vicar's son, he disliked school intensely. His attacks of asthma seemed to pay fortnightly visits and consequently his attendance record was very poor.

When Julia started at the same school she did so very cheerfully, but in common with a great many children who attended there her health went downhill, and she was off with repeated feverish colds. They were obliged to do P.E. in an extremely cold hall, with bare feet and stripped to the waist. I was to learn more of the wretched set-up at the school six years later. At the time I deplored, with other parents, that nothing was done to improve the heating, and that appeals to the headmistress to allow the children to be reasonably dressed in view of the low temperatures fell on deaf ears. As children born three months earlier in the year were in fact having the 'advantage' of a year longer in the school I was afraid that Julia would lose ground through repeated illnesses.

Neither she nor Christopher seemed to have any proper grounding in the tool subjects. They made their letters very badly and told me it didn't matter. I thought sadly of the sound methods used in my old school and of the pleasure the children had in mastering the rudiments. In a short conversation with the headmistress I discovered she had not trained as an infants' teacher and had very few on her staff who had. She had been recommended to apply for the post of headmistress as that was the quickest way to promotion and top salaries, although it was very obvious that she had no real love of young children and they never showed any affection for her.

When Chris was seven the alarm was spread that no boys from the area would be allowed into the local grammar schools in three years' time. A huge comprehensive school was to be built for them in the middle of an estate notorious for car thieves and sex offences. The parents were up in arms and protested violently, but the councillor to whom they appealed said the boys from our area would be needed to form the top stream at the proposed comprehensive.

We decided to try and get Chris into the prep school of the old grammar school – a school with a good name, but right on the other side of the city. It meant two bus journeys each way and much queuing in rush hours excepting when a neighbour was able to take him with his own son. The traffic congestion was so bad that H. could not do the double journey and be back in time for the morning surgery.

However, Chris was able to pass the entrance exam and he was very happy in the capable hands of the headmaster, his wife and staff at the prep school.

In the main school the buildings were old, dirty and badly heated. Dust blew up through the floor boards, the heating apparatus in the baths was broken more often than not, and his old asthma was stirred up constantly with one thing and another. The specialist tried everything under the sun, but his attendance record was down to fifty per cent when he was eleven. It was suggested that he was picking up germs in overcrowded buses, and chills whilst queuing for them. It might help if he could transfer to a school nearer home where he could walk or at least cycle.

There had been a grammar school built after all, and Chris's old school friends were there in spite of all the scares about the comprehensive. We were torn about moving him. He'd made friends and didn't want to move, but we knew he'd never make the grade unless he could keep in better health. We moved him and no doubt the two mile walk improved his health. The school was much cleaner, but he missed his friends and was labelled a snob for speaking the Queen's English. It took him ages to settle down, but he eventually became bi-lingual and spoke the ugly local dialect sufficiently well to be acceptable.

Anthea was leading them a dance at the girls' school at the far side of the city. Like the old Grammar School it had a good reputation, but they didn't seem able to lick her into shape any more than I had been. Her reputation there was sadly akin to the one she gained at the Nursing Home where she was born.

Julia was travel sick from the earliest days and we knew she couldn't cope with long bus journeys. A new High School had been built a few years after the school Chris now attended. There was an extremely efficient Headmistress there and it was within walking or cycling distance. We put her down for it and she eventually went there.

Apart from childish ailments and Chris's more wearying condition I think their childhood days were happy ones. We kept open house and open garden to all the other children in Pemberton Green, and progressed from large moss gardens occupying the front porch to dens under the bushes and trees. Tree climbing and dogged endurance-test attempts at camping and being totally independent followed later. When the latter was going on Chris and his pal trailed into the incinerator corner to do their cooking and back with smoke-reddened eyes, singed hair and pathetic charred-on-the-outside and raw-in-the-middle sausages. They wore themselves to grimy shadows. I looked in at night with mugs of cocoa and substantial snacks and said supper didn't count. They weren't sure that it was ethical, but they drank and gobbled gratefully and slept like the dead.

Not so when another lad begged to sleep in the tent on the lawn. He woke us at about five-thirty in the morning tearing round the lawn and laughing like mad. He was up the beech tree by the gate in his pyjamas later on, and gave the postman a fright. We decided he was not our favourite garden lodger, although he and his sister were almost members of the family.

Chris adored slices of stale toast plastered with butter. He called them 'snackerels' and I kept them in the drop-leaf cupboard of the kitchen cabinet. He was terribly thin, and his long arm often preceded him into the kitchen as he reached for the snackerels to keep the wolf at bay. The neighbours' children became as fond of them as he was, so I had to make plenty of extra toast in case one came in and made eyes at the cabinet.

The apple trees were a source of great joy and to me a great deal of hard work. Their beauty in the spring was usually followed ultimately by a terrific

Author with Anthea in Trafalgar Square.

crop of huge apples – especially from the cooking apple trees. The dessert apple crop varied, but those trees leaned over the next door drive and were a great attraction to children visiting the park.

I cannot bear waste, so all the fallen apples were gathered and sent to various families along the road. When it was time to harvest them we filled every available receptacle and Julia and her crony would often sit at the gate and sell them – all proceeds to the N.S.P.C.C. I sold cookers at threepence a pound and the others at sixpence, and we did a roaring trade. Making apple ginger became an established custom, and again I sold it for the N.S.P.C.C. If we could pick a few blackberries I made some jelly. It was a very hectic time, but I felt guilty if any went bad and had to be thrown away.

The ladies and children of Pemberton Green became very much involved in working for the N.S.P.C.C. Our minister came to see us one day and told us he'd been asked if he could suggest a suitable lady in the district to begin a ladies' committee for the N.S.P.C.C. I asked him not to look at me. I was by this time a class leader at the Methodist Church and a choir member there. After having opened the first fund-raising effort for the newly formed T.G. group I had been drawn into the choir there and subsequently taken over the job of conductor. Membership of the T.G. involved other commitments and with three children my days were not exactly empty.

The minister did look at me and said, 'No, I'm not pushing you to do it, but you know a lot of people and I'm new here. Can you suggest someone? They like their committees very mixed as to social strata and denominational attachments and so on, in order to spread their net as widely as possible.'

I said that the chairman of the local T.G. was the most suitable person, and gave him her name to pass on to the N.S.P.C.C. office. 'Don't mention my name,' I said. 'She's a busy woman and a great friend of mine.'

In a week or two of course, I was invited along with other members of the T.G. and people of the various churches to meet at my friend's. She had agreed to call together a group of ladies, but not to being chairman of an N.S.P.C.C. committee. However, yet another friend and neighbour was induced to take on the chairmanship, and the local committee was launched.

It was to prove an extremely active and successful committee, and from then on we arranged dances, coffee mornings, concerts and so on, and Copperfield was used for garden parties. It was always awful weather immediately prior to the garden parties. We hired a small marquee for the stalls one year, and the first time we were given permission to put up the stalls in a temporary church hall a little way down the road. On that occasion the crowds poured into the garden and had their refreshments and watched the dancing in brilliant sunshine. Very few people could be persuaded to trot along the road and look at the stalls. After that we prepared for the worst, but usually had the marquee sides up and did a roaring trade. The committee were terrific workers and we served refreshments for anything up to two hundred. The very idea of a garden party seemed to draw people from far and near.

Coco the clown was a personal friend of one member of the committee and was staying in his caravan whilst doing a road-safety campaign in the city. He came along at very short notice and opened one garden party. We had to tell people not to talk about it outside the area, as I knew we could not cope with the numbers who would have turned up. Our resources were at stretching point, but we coped. A Scots piper in full rig played for the team of dancers we had the same afternoon, and although it was a bit blowy the rain kept off again.

Just before that particular event an Irish lady came to the door and asked if I wanted a team of Irish dancers for the garden party. I thanked her and explained that we had a Scottish team booked, but suggested that she might see the chairman and give her all the details in case we arranged an event later on. The dances we'd had for our main winter effort were becoming more and more expensive to put on, and we were scratching our heads over what to do for a change. I remembered the Irish lady and suggested that we put on an Irish evening.

'What's an Irish evening?' they asked very suspiciously.

'Well,' I floundered, 'we've had an offer of a team of dancers, we could get some Irish singers. Everybody loves Irish songs. We could put on special Irish refreshments and I've heard of an excellent young elocutionist of Irish extraction . . .' They were not convinced, but gradually warmed to the idea.

We had an ex-domestic science teacher who produced Irish recipes. Irish cheese was ordered, our expert flower arranger did a beautiful green and white arrangement in the porch of the hall and the lady who had conjured up Coco produced gallons of delicious Irish broth. The entertainment side was left to me.

Two of my friends in the church and T.G. choir promised to sing solos and trios with me. My choir pianist offered to come and an earlier pianist, now going downhill with cancer, was thrilled to make long playing tapes of innumerable Irish tunes to play as background music.

I went to call on the lady who had quite unwittingly triggered off the whole thing, and found her out but a houseful of children. I went back later and booked not only the dancers but two 'splendid real Irish tenors'. I was very pleased.

The mother of the young elocutionist was doubtful whether her daughter could help. She was working for her G.C.E. and was very busy. 'Anyway,' she said, 'I've never heard of an Irish evening. What is it?' She was even more suspicious than the committee members. I tried to explain. 'And who do you think can make soda bread in this place?' she asked indignantly. I said a member of the committee was a domestic science teacher. 'I don't care what she is. If she's not Irish she can't make soda bread! Now I've got a friend who *can* make it. How much will you need? She'll make your bread if I ask her.'

I was a bit non-plussed, but an excellent scrounger by this time, and I never turned down an offer if I could use it. 'Well, that would be extremely kind, but we'd need enough for up to two hundred to have with the Gaelic broth we're serving.'

'Humph,' she answered. 'I'll let you know.'

The lady whose services had been promised was ill in the end, but the committee members did their stuff. The young girl came – a most intelligent girl – and had everyone entranced by her poems.

But of course it *was* an Irish evening and it couldn't possibly have passed without alarms and excursions. Sadly for me they happened at my end of the room and in my department. The refreshments were greatly appreciated and the committee did wonders in the small kitchen attached to the big church hall we'd hired. It was designed primarily for producing coffee and biscuits, and serving the hot broth produced some problems.

My pianist and lady singers turned up in good time. The friend who had offered to see to the amplification of the taped background music turned up, but the team of dancers came in penny numbers and without their teacher. She'd got married earlier in the day. They thought someone else was seeing to the music for their dancing. Records were produced and turned out to be the wrong ones. A tape recording was finally hunted down at the eleventh hour and we had a frantic playing through to pin-point the dances they thought they knew. Their mothers saw them into their splendid costumes and I left them in a back room desperately practising their routine. I was anxious about my two tenors. They hadn't come.

In the meantime the guests were turning up and settling down happily, humming and tapping to the tunes played over the amplifier. The area organizer for the N.S.P.C.C. had come. He was Irish, all charm, and delighted by all that had been arranged.

I watched the doorway and finally two gentleman sailed in radiating bonhomie and a strong smell of ale. My tenors had made it after all. They were led across the hall and introduced to me behind the stage curtain. I asked what they were singing, and they were very vague. They had between them one piece of sheet music with the back half torn off. 'Oh,' they assured me, 'the pianist will know everything we sing. She can just vamp on the piano.' My pianist is an excellent sight reader, but feels herself inadequate as a vamper. We finally nailed them down and found their repertoire was overlapping with the ladies'. This meant changing the ladies' songs for others we could find accompaniments for. Fortunately, no one in the room minded the delay, excepting me. I was getting hot under the collar and everywhere else, but we finally drew back the curtains and began.

It all went off like a dream up to half time. Then I discovered the local press had sent a photographer. He took some marvellous pictures of the dancers, whilst the committee ladies flew round serving refreshments. I had sent complimentary tickets to the families of the entertainers, and the father of the huge family was sitting at a table near the platform with his wife and several younger children. He was very hungry and I kept sending someone to fill up his soup bowl and take more soda bread and cheese. The mother of the elocutionist was there – obviously delighted at her daughter's reception and very warm in her praise of whoever had made the soda bread after all.

The plates were cleared away and we began the second half of the concert with a very gay atmosphere, but to my dismay I discovered my two tenors had disappeared. They had scorned our broth and hopped off to the local again. We had to be out of the hall by ten o'clock and I daren't hold up the proceedings. However, as the children finished their second lot of dancing a muted cheer from the back of the hall reached my ears. The two well-oiled tenors were back – in the finest fettle. The audience cheered them up the room and they came up the platform steps beaming like the sun. Yorkshire eyes were smiling along with the Irish ones as everyone joined in the last choruses.

People were asking months later when we were going to have another Irish evening. The charming N.S.P.C.C. organizer said he'd never seen such a skilful chairman and that if we hadn't made a penny for the Society's funds we'd done a great deal for international relations. I told him I'd never had quite such a rocky boat to sail nor been more thankful to see it safely to shore. We had in fact made a tidy profit. We never kept a record of the wear and tear on my nervous system.

For a number of years our committee organized a party for a group of the casework children. We fetched some of them in cars and provided eats and presents and arranged a simple entertainment. Between them the committee members had a fair number of children, and one year it was suggested that they might put on a concert for the little guests. I offered to organize it and see what talents and costumes we could dig up.

It was unfortunate that at that time I was having a good deal of menopausal trouble, and had to keep repairing to bed. It so happened that I was in such a plight on the first Saturday when all the children had been asked to come. I won't let children down if it can possibly be avoided so I arranged for Anthea to give them orange juice and biscuits in the drawing room whilst I had them upstairs a few at a time to make a note of their ages and potential as entertainers. The youngest was three or four and the oldest about fifteen. Chris played the cello, Andrew the clarinet, several recorders. Some could dance, some recite and Julia and Alison were young enough to warm to the idea of dressing up in dirty jeans and singing 'The Hippopotamus Song'. The only costumes they had between them were for a robin, a witch and a mandarin.

I told them I'd work out what I could and see them all later on. We had one star pianist to highlight the proceedings.

Then began a very busy time for me. It gave me a great deal of pleasure and passed away days when I was confined to bed again. I wrote a rhyming playlet called 'The Robin, The Witch and the Mandarin', and several poems to suit the younger children. One for two little sisters who were very much alike called 'Not Quite Twins', and one for a little Scots boy about a dog called 'Marc' and so on.

For the older boys I wrote, 'Time Was' – a crazy play about cavemen and woad and the Common Market. The same boys were to dress up in top hats and dicky bows and be a jazz band. Linking all the items I wrote a play called 'Gran's Album', in which a child and her granny talk about the photographs and then see them come to life. The second half was all nativity scenes, and I got the children to record their own taped music and singing for the tableaux. Anthea was a capable stage-manager. I had them in groups to rehearse on Saturdays and many gallons of orange juice were drunk in between. For a final rehearsal we borrowed the Methodist hall, but I was ill again, and had an awful job to see it through.

On the night of the party there was a terrible gale and the bus bringing the casework children to the hall was very late. The driver had lost his way. Our little actors and actresses were getting more and more excited and restive behind the scenes. Alison, looking a terrible sight ready to sing, 'Mud, mud, glorious mud', could not be kept out of sight. She escaped into the hall where a surprising number of people had paid to see the concert. A lady on the front row said, 'Fancy anyone letting a child come out to a concert in a state like that!' Alison was delighted and came pushing back-stage to tell us the joke.

The little waifs were finally ushered in by the N.S.P.C.C. Officers and we began our concert. In the interval we gave them loads of beautiful food.

As we made ten pounds for the Society's funds as well, we thought it had been worth all the effort. Someone suggested we should do it again the following week, but many of the nativity scene costumes had been borrowed from the Methodist church and were needed for their Christmas mime. It was too near Christmas and I was too tired to face it all again, but we'd had enormous fun, and many people had been impressed by the talents displayed.

The following year it was obvious that a major 'op' was inevitable, and I was whisked off to hospital towards summer.

My loyal 'Friday' lady, who had come for several years had had her husband ill and he had always resented the fact that she had come more often than originally planned. We parted company very regretfully. I knew I'd miss her singing and cheerful face as much as her practical help. I advertised in a local shop and one morning Mrs McFee came to the back door – careworn, late forty-ish.

She sat in the corner and looked me straight in the eye. 'I'd better come clean,' she said. I wondered what revelations I was in for. I carried on with my ironing and listened to her sad and fascinating story.

Her mother had kept a lodging house, but didn't like housework, so Cath and her sisters were up at dawn and working hard all the evening after school. She had in fact, worked very hard ever since she could remember. It wasn't much of a life, endless scrubbing, meal making and bed changing. Cath married fairly young. Her first-born, a son, was an epileptic and a constant anxiety. Her second child was a bright girl with some physical problems which cleared up eventually. Her husband developed galloping consumption and died. With two youngsters she was more or less driven to going back home, where her mother left her in charge and went off to work in a factory, which she much preferred.

A certain Sandy McFee, a huge fellow, was a fairly regular frequenter of the boarding house and he showed a great interest in Cath's two youngsters. They became fond of him and in the end he and Cath hitched up. They managed eventually to get a council house as she had the two children. Sandy was a most devoted husband and they were a very happy family. They had a son and daughter of their own, and Cath's daughter by her first husband made a 'good' marriage at nineteen and went off to live in a desirable residence provided by her well-to-do in-laws.

Sandy was often away for a night or two, as he was a transport driver, but when he was at home he would not stir without his family. But a change came over him and his contentment seemed to drain away, replaced by an anxiety Cath had never seen before. After one trip up north he vanished.

At this point in her tale Cath lost control. 'I just can't accept it. We never had a wrong word. He adored the kids. It doesn't make sense. I'll never rest till I've found out why. Bottom's gone out of my world. I've always had a hard life, but we were real happy. It's not like him. I'm sorry. I didn't mean to break down, but you'd have heard from somebody if I hadn't told you. That's my story. I'm on Public Assistance, but I'm allowed to earn a bit more. I could walk here easy and I'd like to come if you can accept me now you know everything. But I've not finished with Sandy. My kids want their dad, and I'll find him if it's the last thing I do.'

I agreed to take her on, and in no time she was almost a member of the family. I kept a little moss garden in a large dish on top of the little wall by the back door. It was full of lavender sprigs and rambler roses when she first came, and she said that she'd wanted very much to work for me as soon as she saw the little garden. Her special line was animals. She had a huge dog, a cat and a budgie and they all slept happily together on her hearth.

The children liked her. She had a raucous voice which she raised in cheerful but toneless song as she scrubbed the steps and polished the little wall and the red tiles in the porch. The noise was almost a parody of a broken musical hall singer and reduced Christopher to tears of mirth.

Her sad story continued some time after her advent to Copperfield. She heard from some old friend that he'd seen Sandy somewhere. She went to the police and begged them to find him, but apparently they said they couldn't arrest him for deserting her. She decided to go to Scotland and hunt out his half-sisters and see if he'd been hiding up there.

I was very anxious about the trip, convinced in my own mind that she would uncover something explosive.

When she came back she was in a terrible state. From the sisters she learnt that he had been born out of wedlock and had run away at the age of sixteen. At nineteen he had married a 'bad un' who had been off with the soldiers at the nearby barracks as soon as they were married. He had been desperately unhappy and eventually gone away. His wife had been living with someone and borne him two or three children. They didn't know where Sandy was, but it was obvious that his marriage to Cath was bigamous.

Cath reported to the police. Now they could act. He could leave her with two children to support, but bigamy was a criminal offence. They set to work and found him. He was charged, but allowed bail, which a friend paid. Whilst on bail he worked on a construction site which had an old bus as a make-shift canteen. Going up the steps one day into the bus his great weight caused a step to break and he fell over backwards and broke his back.

Cath went to court and saw her huge, devoted Sandy a broken man in every sense. He wept and said his only happy days had been with her and the children, but he'd seen someone he'd known in Scotland and got a feeling he was being followed. He daren't tell Cath he'd another wife, and all he could think of doing was disappearing.

He had to serve a sentence, but his words in court had made her heart bleed for him. 'I still love him,' she told me. 'He loves us. I shall take him back and look after him when he comes out.' She kept her word. Her mother and daughter and one of her sisters cut her dead after that. It broke her heart that she was not allowed to see her little granddaughter, but Sandy got a divorce and they were legally man and wife. The epileptic boy married a half-witted girl and poor Cath was landed with providing the wedding breakfast. A born coper, she explained to me that the girl's family were a poor lot and she couldn't let her lad down. She got everything ready 'but the last little destructions' before they went off to the church, and it all 'went lovely'. The last I heard of the bride and groom was that they had a young family the girl was incapable of caring for, and Cath was doing what she could for them.

Sandy's back never healed properly, but in spite of a coronary Cath is still working hard as a doctor's caretaker and part-time receptionist, and Sandy is hobbling about in the background. Their two children are happily married. What a woman! One of the finest I've met.

I must add that in the days of their prosperity she had had a great weakness for hats. It was her invariable cure for depression to buy a new one. When they moved house on one occasion she went to the shop where she'd bought most of them and told the friend who ran the shop that she'd fifty-seven hats – many of them worn only once. The friend said, 'Bring them back. I'll put new trimmings on.' 'Well,' said Cath to me. 'It's a pity to waste good hats.' I had given her a rather special bottle-green velvet hat to wear when she went to court. She certainly wore it with an air, and it suited her immensely.

After my hysterectomy we took our first trip abroad. H., Chris and Julia were mad on boating holidays. We had spent our first one on the Cam and the Ouse in a houseboat called the *Rajah*. As years go it must have been Wasp Year. Julia was not a fearful child over anything excepting wasps. She set up a high-pitched shriek every time she saw one. I called them the Gentry and tried to pretend I didn't loathe the blighters as much as Julia did. As soon as I began to prepare a meal dozens of them flew through the tiny galley window to keep me company. If I didn't want them I had to cook in the four foot square with the window shut. The loo door opened into the galley. It was virtually impossible to use the loo without leaving the door open to accommodate one's feet in the same. The tiny wash bowl collected more scum in an hour than I was used to coping with in a month with our good soft water at home. Foraging meant tying up as early as possible and beetling off swiftly to the nearest dairy in order to buy the special milk before it was all sold. Ordinary milk went sour very quickly. A heavy mahogany table had to be lugged out on to the deck from the saloon so that H. and I could make up our bunks for the night – not much fun when it threw it down.

When the moon rose on one side and the sun set on the other – both reflected in the water – and there was no sound but light water lapping and the munching of horses on the banks it was a wonderful experience. Feeding swans in a bed of water lilies at dawn was another, but I wondered if I was quite right in the head when I battled with the Gentry in a boiling hot, smelly gallery whilst Julia shrieked from the saloon that another one had got in there. The next two years H. took Chris and Julia boating, and expressed his surprise at the amount of dirt that collected everywhere. Anthea and I went with her friend and Althea to France one year and the next I went alone to Scotland. I had tried in vain to lure H. there. That year the three sailors had had very rough weather and some anxious times. It had been wickedly cold and wet throughout the country.

In '63 we decided to go to Wales, but couldn't book single rooms for Chris and Julia. On impulse we went into Cook's and succeeded in booking for the four of us on a boat in Holland. It was a very enjoyable holiday and awoke my spouse's interest in overseas travel at last.

Julia went to the High School that autumn and I was without a child in the house from breakfast to tea time for the first time for eighteen years. Looking back I think some of my despondency was just the aftermath of the major operation. There was an acute shortage of teachers – particularly trained infants' teachers – and appeals were being made constantly for women to help, if only for an odd session or two. I knew that the situation at the nearest infants' school was desperate, and also that the physical conditions were bad. Huts had been put up as temporary classrooms, and the staff were always leaving. I was very torn. Parents kept telling me how anxious they were about their children. I felt very mean to live so near and not help out.

CHAPTER THIRTEEN

WHERE ANGELS FEAR TO TREAD

O ne day I decided to ring up the Education Office and see if they were interested in my offer to help. Little did I dream what I had triggered off!

I was told that the local school was the most difficult in the city to keep staffed and that there was a group of four to five year olds who had no teacher on two afternoons, one teacher for the mornings and another for three afternoons. I agreed to take them on the two afternoons when they had no teacher, and to go two mornings to play for assembly and hymn practice, take singing and coach some backward readers. I was pretty hot stuff on teaching singing and reading and thought I would be able to cope.

H. was afraid I'd find it too much so soon after my operation, but having decided to try I would not look back. I began on one of the mornings. The head asked me to take a class whose teacher hadn't turned up, and I sallied forth with a bunch of keys to do my first teaching for nineteen years. The keys I'd been given were the wrong ones, and the children crowded in, wet through, whilst I struggled in vain to open the desk and find something to mark the register. By the time I'd been across the flooded yard to get the right keys from the headmistress and then found there were no red biros nor pencils in the desk drawer I was getting hot under the collar. However, I finally got things sorted out and saw that the class was well-handled and used to a good routine. I learnt later that their teacher earned a mere pittance, as she was officially a nursery assistant. She had been promised a chance to train, but along with others taken on when the schools were desperate she had never been given the opportunity to improve her status. She had learnt sound teaching methods from an older sister who was a trained teacher and from my own observations – and I eventually went into every class in the school – she was a most capable and reliable infants' teacher.

The next afternoon I turned up in good time in order to be spared a 'wrong keys' fiasco. I was told that my room was used for dinners, as the new dining room wasn't finished yet. I had to stack the dinner tables and exchange them for the children's working tables, which were out in one of the cloakrooms. It was horsework, and I was still toiling away when the mob arrived. I say 'mob' because these children had been in the hands of no fewer than ten different teachers during their first term at school. They were as wild as could be. The Beatles were the rage, and the Methodist minister's little boy was at the front of the crowd who pushed in shouting, 'She loves me, yah, yah, yah'. One wore a plastic Beatle wig and they were all Beatle mad. They were delighted to have a teacher on Wednesday afternoons. The more timid had been in the habit of going to another classroom and crying, 'Where are we to go today?' On Friday the headmistress had said that they did activities before playtime, and asked me to clear the room before the last session and to have all three classes in our block for a good sing until home time.

Activities consisted of drawing here, plasticine there, water play somewhere else, building bricks, painting, Wendy-housing and so on. One boy was MD and went into the Wendy house to show himself off to the little girls, or tipped over the paint pots of the artists or scribbled across chalkers who were busy in a cloud of pink and blue chalk dust in one corner. Bedlam was not in it!

Ten minutes before play we began a big clear-up and put away, and the chaos was even greater. I tried to stack the tables to clear the room ready for the ninety children to crowd in for the 'sing-song'. There had been no effort to keep tables of one size and type in each room, and the tables which looked the same had subtle differences which made stacking impossible. I'd six different types of table when I finally got them sorted out. There was disintegrating coconut matting near the teacher's desk for the children to sit on for story telling. I rolled the mats up to put them in the middle of the room for the singing session, and found half an inch of dust and coconut fibre underneath. By the time I'd swept that up playtime was over, and I was an absolute rag. The other two teachers in the block thankfully brought their children in and we squashed the ninety into the room before the teachers went back to their rooms to clear up in peace and end the day calmly.

I staggered home and lay flat on my back on the lounge floor. I couldn't believe that this was called teaching. No wonder the staff wouldn't stay.

When my mornings ran according to schedule I played the piano in the hall for the first half hour or more. The temperature was often forty-two degrees or under. The children came across a badly-drained yard with their shoes soaking and then sat on the floor. They coughed and sneezed and were told by the head that it was rude to make a noise during prayers. I almost left the piano and scragged her, remembering as I did Julia's long battle against colds and Christopher's struggles with asthma. There were loud nose-blowing sessions with the head saying, 'Blow harder and get it clear,' and the inevitable ear-troubles following. Staff nearing retirement were off repeatedly with chest troubles and painful rheumatic symptoms. Slightly younger staff attended more regularly but were often in sheepskin coats all day long, and looked perpetually miserable.

There was no staff room. A cramped, unheated passage with a gas stove in had a few chairs along the wall. At break we sat there clutching our coffee and GRUMBLING. It was the tone of the whole place.

More often than not I was acting as supply teacher in the mornings, which meant going to any class whose teacher was absent. Some children saw their own teacher very rarely and never had any of their morning work marked. I was very sorry for them, and found myself marking their sum papers whilst all the rest of the staff were having dinner with the children. I then staggered home and prepared our meal.

The new dining room was finished by the end of my second week. If it had not been I couldn't have carried on. The big furniture upheaval before the afternoon sessions was intolerable.

Once I'd got to know 'my' children – the class I took in the afternoons – a certain amount of law and order was established, and I became very fond of them. They were always noisy, but it was not their fault that they had had such a raw deal. They waited for me at the school gate and gave me a warm welcome. Many of them were patients, and their mothers told H.

they loved it when I was their teacher. We had our own sing-songs and I invented stories to keep them quiet. I was not supposed to be teaching reading or writing, but I slipped bits in and we often had a game of 'Birds' to sharpen up their mental arithmetic. I divided them into groups and gave each group the name of a bird. I then fired questions at them and every correct answer was a mark for their group. They loved it. I introduced letter formation into drawing lessons as patterns for borders and helped the backward readers in the library corner during 'activities'.

When all the staff were there I went from one hut to another in the mornings taking singing lessons. The lessons were short and it meant a frantic moving of tables as often as not. It wasn't so bad in good weather, but in bad I had the problem of putting on my outdoor clothes to charge across the yard. If the room was not ready the time I could spend on singing was often very short, but it was amazing how quickly they learned the songs and what a big repertoire they had. I enjoyed it in spite of the endless chasing about, but it was very exhausting.

The deputy head was a fully-qualified infants' teacher and a very conscientious woman, but it was soon apparent that another member of the staff was after her position. This Mrs Potts and the head between them made life extremely difficult for the younger Miss Grace. Mrs Potts admitted that, like the head, she had trained for older children, but had changed to infants for quick promotion. She added that she would have been guilty of murder if she'd stayed any longer with older children. It was a pity that the one full-time, experienced and qualified infants' teacher should be hounded out of the school by the ambitious Mrs Potts, but that is what happened. Miss Grace benefited really, as she went to be head at a church school with good old-fashioned buildings well-heated. I was sorry to part company with her, but glad for her sake.

Once she was made deputy-head Mrs Potts spent an ever-increasing amount of time in the head's room, and kept finding excuses for me to take on her class. It was obvious they were not being well-taught, and their progress was very poor, considering that most of them were intelligent children from good homes. I was asked to take over Mrs Potts' Friday afternoon playtime duty in addition to my other session earlier in the week.

I then had the room-clearing and table-stacking to do before play in order to fit in the yard duty, and then without a breather cope with the three classes for singing until hometime. I don't mind pulling my weight, but I saw red when I was left with so much to cope with. I had an attack of cystitis and my weariness increased.

Friends whose children were at the school kept asking me to do something about the children having to strip down to a pair of cotton briefs and bare feet before doing P.E. in the very cold hall. In the end I wrote to the Education Officer and said that I should have to pack my job in if the heating could not be improved. The heating engineers were on the spot 'pronto', and the staff rubbed their hands and said they'd got a champion at last. The head was furious with me. The heating system worked in its own time. By the middle of the afternoon when the sun was shining the rooms which had been 40 degrees in the morning were well over 80.

H. said he couldn't understand why so many children at Pemberton Infants' had ear trouble. I said I thought it was the nose-blowing sessions held religiously by the head during assembly. He nearly hit the ceiling. 'The woman must be crazy,' he said. 'Can't you stop it?'

She was not an approachable woman. She was a bundle of nerves and very unsure of herself. Children would offer to go to her with a message and then come back and say they didn't want to go. I decided to approach via Mrs Potts, who enjoyed her confidence. I rang up one evening after two more of my children had gone down with earache, and asked her if she could stop the nose-blowing, as it was dangerous unless done one nostril at a time, and damaged eardrums could be a source of trouble all one's life. She was incredulous, and told me not to talk a lot of poppycock. I then found a text-book dealing specifically with children's diseases, where the point was made very strongly and I took it to school the next day. I showed Mrs Potts and the rest of the staff.

The following afternoon one of the older members of the staff was looking out for me. She called me to her room and said, 'I must warn you. The head has asked the Chief Inspector to come and see you about making trouble on the staff. I'm with you up to the hilt, but keep my name out of it.' One after the other the staff, all but Mrs Potts, came and said they were with me but didn't want to lose their jobs.

Sure enough, I had just got under weigh with my afternoon's work when the head appeared and asked me if I would see Mr Plummer in her office. She said she would keep an eye on the children.

Mr Plummer was a wise and kindly man. He tried to draw me out, and in the end I told him exactly what the situation was like at the school. He asked me why I'd not packed it in like so many of my predecessors. I said there were many children of my friends and neighbours, some of whom were frantic about the conditions, and I had decided to do what I could before departing. 'Besides,' I added, 'I was told I couldn't take it, and I don't like giving in. I love children and can't bear to see them badly handled. The children I teach in the afternoons will be split up if I go, and so will those I'm acting as unofficial supply teacher for in the mornings.'

'Not all schools are like this,' he said. 'Why don't you teach music to older children? You're wasted here. There's a crying need for music teachers.'

I said I would leave at the end of the term and make a determined effort to pass the driving test so that I could travel further afield. He said I should have reported the ear business to the medical officer and that I'd better go and see her.

The prospect did not please. I was trying to keep H. out of it, but he'd brought many of my charges into the world and was very much concerned for their physical welfare.

The schools' chief medical officer was an up-tight Scotswoman. She eyed me with great suspicion and was obviously determined to uphold authority at all costs. She asked what my complaint was. I knew I was speaking on behalf of many young children and their very anxious parents. I didn't give a damn about having another teaching job, but I didn't like making official complaints about the headmistress. I told her what had been happening.

'I expect these young children would be absent a great deal, anyhow,' was her attitude. I told her of the immediate improvement in the health of the youngsters once they left Pemberton Infants'. She was not impressed. She then brought H.'s name into it. 'I expect your husband takes the matter much more lightly than you do. I doubt whether he is much concerned.'

'My husband is very much concerned,' I fired back. 'He is a Guy's man, not a fool,' I said as I opened the door and left her stewing in her warm office. I saw a bit of colour creep into her sallow cheeks as I shut the door.

H. roared with laughter. 'Absolutely typical of the breed,' was his comment. 'Oh well, you've done your best. Get out at the end of the term. Those teachers should walk out when the rooms are so cold. Factory workers wouldn't put up with such conditions, but women will not let children down as long as they can stand on their feet.'

To my surprise Mr Plummer came again. I was teaching a class in the morning – my music was almost non-existent by that time, as the two oldest staff members were off so much. The head came over for me and stayed with the children. I went back to her little room with two heaters on full blast. Mr Plummer was very friendly. I had a feeling he'd heard of my interview with the medical officer and had approved of my handling of the lady. 'I suppose you're still doing supply teaching over there?' he asked, nodding towards the block I'd just left. I said that was so. He chatted away and I knew the head would be half dead with cold. I had to start removing my thick outdoor coat and then my woolly. He seemed to be amused. 'You're not cold in here?' he asked. I said I was afraid the head would be shivering and she had arthritis. He wasn't moved. 'Go and see the chief music inspector. I'll tell him to expect you. They need help with music all over the city.' I said I'd have a rest first and then try and pass the driving test. We parted on the best of terms.

The next day – late in the afternoon – the medical officer appeared. She asked to see the heating system in the cold block, but the rooms were very hot by that time. The thermostat was in a small room, but the coldest place in the whole school was the big hall where we began the day. With so much glass on sunny days it was sweltering by afternoon.

A confab, with the head followed, and until the end of term the staff were invited to take their coffee and afternoon tea in the head's little room. Mrs Potts and the head kept on looking at me as if they couldn't believe anyone would dare to question their joint authority. The old staff members said the head had been hauled before the chief education officer, but I found that hard to swallow. At any rate there was an end to the noisy blowing sessions and the children were told to cover one nostril when clearing the other. The heating engineers had another go, but I'm told things are still not right. The new head has shown some concern and tried to improve conditions, but according to one staff member I meet occasionally it is still not a happy place. Another teacher told me the unhappiest days of her life were spent there.

I left after four terms – a wiser and sadder woman.

* * *

Driving a car was not something nature designed me for. Ten years previously H. had tried to persuade me to take the test. It was not that I couldn't drive, but I was reduced to a jelly when being tested. My left ear had begun to make its own noises when I was carrying Julia. It had become increasingly deaf. My right ear compensated by being increasingly sensitive. I could always hear conversations not meant for me on my right side and never hear confidences on my left. This didn't help when I first took the test. The dour man testing me had an accent, and I had to drive with the window on my right open, as at that time one had to wave one's arm about like a lunatic in addition to giving automatic signals. The first instruction he gave me I didn't hear at all – thanks to the noise of traffic through the open window, and a pneumatic drill. He repeated it testily and we got off to a bad start. I failed, of course, and the fellow who had instructed me consoled me by saying, 'That miserable beggar never passes anybody first time.'

The next time a nice little man tested me, but I was not well, and had had news of two deaths that morning. He asked me why I was so jumpy, and said I could drive, but was a bundle of nerves. He failed me.

Much later I was recommended to go to an instructor who was very pleasant. He just kept saying, 'You can drive all right. No need to worry.' I was hoping he'd really drill me. He was fat, the car was small and I had to look down before grabbing the clutch in case I got hold of his fat knee. His cigarette smoke poisoned me. When I failed the test for the third time the instructor was very angry. I thought he was going to attack the examiner. 'You can drive. He must be mad, the miserable blighter,' he said. After that I decided to give up – until the end of my four terms at Pemberton Infants'.

My troubles there had raised the fighter in me.

I saw a Fiat 500 in the local garage and decided I was sure I could drive a car as small as that. I bought it, to H.'s consternation.

'Where are you going to put it? You can't keep a car if you've not passed the test. You *would* have to do a thing like that!'

I answered, 'If I've got a car I shall jolly well have to pass the test. We'll put up a car port round the back of the house. There's plenty of room, and it won't block the drive if you have to take a night call.'

'I can't understand your mind. The last thing in the world I would do would be to buy a car when I'd not passed the test and I'd nowhere to keep it,' he went on.

'You're not me! I shall feel such a fool if I fail next time I'll make sure I don't, and I'm having none of your fat cigarette smoking, conceited little instructors. I've seen a good book in the library. I'll follow the drill in there.'

We got two funny little men to put up a car port. What it lacked in grace it made up in durability. A friend came out and helped to drill me, and I decided to take the test in another town to break the spell. The examiner was a gentleman – he actually addressed me by name and opened the door for me to get in the car. I just couldn't believe it. He examined me very thoroughly and eventually passed me. I nearly hugged him. It was ten years since my first attempt. I was jubilant.

I rang up the Education Office and was eventually linked up with the man in charge of music. He asked to see me and made an appointment. I turned up on time, but Mr Hind was missing. He shared a secretary with Mr Plummer, who eventually emerged from his office and apologised for his colleague's absence. 'He is probably visiting a school. Can you wait for half an hour?' He asked the secretary to fetch me a cup of tea, and I began my vigil. I set four o'clock as my dead-line, as I didn't want to be late for my family's homecoming. Mr Hind came dashing in just as his secretary was preparing to leave and I'd decided to go home. He was covered with confusion. He'd been so thrilled listening to some infants singing that he'd forgotten the time.

He had the reputation for being pleasant, but extremely scatter-brained, and he lived up to it all the time I knew him.

He was thrilled to hear of my experience as a singer and conductor and that I was a qualified teacher. Apparently it was rare to find all three. He took down some details and said he would give me a ring. I think he then lost his bit of paper, but some time later he rang me up and asked if I would go and see the headmaster of Bishop Bank with a view to taking over the singing teaching there.

That opened the door to a very happy and rewarding period in my life.

I drove my little red car through the school gates and parked it amongst several more. A number of children watched me with interest. When I got out and asked if they could tell me where Mr Stroller would be they all offered to take me to him. I knew at once that it was a happy school and a complete contrast to Pemberton Infants, where the children would not approach the head if they could avoid it.

I laughed at their enthusiasm and said one child would do, but two more tagged on and escorted me to Mr Stroller's open door. That door was always open, and the kind-hearted man who ran the school was the most approachable person I've ever met.

CHAPTER FOURTEEN

STILL WATERS AND TROUBLED

He was entertaining a very fat, good-natured bobby. The school was constantly being broken into, and the two men were obviously old friends. I introduced myself, and within five minutes felt completely at home. Mr Stroller took me round the school and introduced me to all the staff. From the expressions on the faces of the staff and children it was plain that he was welcome. They all seemed very pleased that they would be having regular singing lessons. It was arranged that I should go on two afternoons and fit in all the school with half hour lessons. This meant 'doubling up' the oldest children. Eighty at a time if the children were all there.

There were sets of books for each age group and it meant sharing books when there were two classes taken together. The children were streamed, and I had the A and B streams in one big group and later the C streams – always smaller classes. The contrast was very marked. The C children read very badly and behaved extremely badly. They were very hard work and yet they enjoyed their lessons, were always impatient to rush into the hall and difficult to persuade to leave at the end of their lessons. Their hard-working teachers had a breather whilst I took them, and I felt they should have been on double salary.

The A and B children could be restless, especially in windy weather, but once they knew a song they sang with great gusto. The Oxford books were marvellously well-graded, with basic music theory included. When I'd had a child throughout his four years in the school he knew at least two hundred songs and carols from all over the world, and, if he'd any brain at all, the elements of music. Their hands shot up continuously asking for favourite songs, and I was so thrilled to hear them asking for Grieg's 'Last Spring' or Handel and Mozart as often as sea-shanties.

I did not like the very big classes, and eventually I was allowed an extra morning session so that I could play for assembly and take all the classes individually. The senior assistant said we ought to have a choir, so one session was booked for a choir practice. Choosing the children was one of the most difficult things I ever did. Every child in the top two classes wanted to be in the choir. We'd decided to have twenty or twenty-four children. I had to choose them from eighty, and there were tears amongst some I had to refuse.

It was a great joy to have the picked voices in a reasonable group – all of them good readers. We had a marvellous time at choir practices, and several of our boys were persuaded to join the church choirs in the city. Unfortunately the finest singer I had was from a poor home and proved very unreliable over attending the church choir rehearsals. Another from a very different home quickly became a prized soloist in the city parish church.

During my first few terms at Bishop Bank I had the help of a gracious lady, who offered her services as pianist just after I'd been asked to take the singing lessons. She was not always able to come, but it made things easier for me when I could face the children all the time instead of sitting at the upright piano. We had some very happy hours together, and the children missed her as much as I did when eventually she was unable to come.

After my first few terms there I was approached by Mr Hind and asked if I would take over a group of girls at a certain secondary modern school. The school was notorious and at first I refused. Before that I had been asked if I would spend one morning at an old school in a very down-town district. It was a mixed senior school and the area was gradually being taken over by immigrants. I had never taught seniors and doubted my ability to manage them, but the headmaster showed me a room with a piano in, which he said could be mine, and a brand new beautiful piano in the hall. He said they were desperate to have some music in the school. I looked at the squalid surroundings and the unhappy faces of many of the children. They lived in back-to-back houses which faced streets choked with traffic at busy times. There was not a blade of grass in sight. I remembered my own free childhood with trees and fields all round, music in the home and at church, and I felt bound to try and bring a bit of music into their lives.

I began there on a January morning, driving through the rush hour in my decrepit little car, and taking a wrong turning in the jungle of streets half a mile from the school. It was sleeting, and my inside was tied in knots after coping with rush-hour traffic for the first time.

Assembly was over when I finally staggered into the school. The teacher whose room I had been promised had not been told, and she was not overjoyed at having to move all her tackle out at a moment's notice.

My classes included one of mainly non-English-speaking Pakistanis. They were all boys – several much above normal school age. They eyed me in a way which made my blood curdle. Fortunately their number included two English-speaking intelligent Hindu boys. I talked to them about rhythm and got them interested and co-operating, and eventually trying to sing some songs from the National Song Book.

Another small class of boys were very high-spirited and ragged me as much as they dared. They were terrified of the head – an unpleasant gorilla of a Jew – and I threatened to send them to him. 'No, not John, Mrs Ta-té,' they said. 'We'll be good, only don't send us to John.' This John turned up at the end of assembly and used a heavy cane on the hands of anyone reported to him. There were shrieks of agony from the lads he punished and I wouldn't have sent them to him. Assembly was taken by the deputy head, of whom the children were very fond. He was an easy-going, pleasant man, a bachelor, very patient and probably the kindest person those children ever met.

Compared with Bishop Bank, which was situated in a big field, had rose bushes and cherry trees inside the gates and very pleasant rooms attractively decorated, the senior school was extremely underprivileged. The trouble was the bigger classes. I had two with mainly local children and a group of non-English-speaking girls. The combination was terrible. The teachers who handed them over to me were often dead-white and shaking as they did so, and the children were often fighting as they came through the door.

Looking back I don't know how I stuck it out for two terms. I taught them as much theory as they were capable of taking in, and they enjoyed clapping rhythms. I took old radio lesson pamphlets to give them some variety in the songs, and they loved cowboy songs and any with exciting rhythms. One young teacher (who was leaving as soon as possible and didn't care if he finished up sweeping the streets) used to tiptoe through the room to me and whisper, 'Three Gypsies', every week. We always sang it for him, and it seemed to satisfy the children as well as soothe his tattered nerves.

The head came in one day when the older immigrants were doing their best. He was delighted that I'd got them singing. 'Will they sing any of their own songs?' he asked. I told him they had done so once or twice. 'Come out and sing for me,' he ordered them. They refused. It had taken me a long time to get them happy and relaxed enough to sing for me. He got very angry and the situation was very tricky. In the end I coaxed them and they went out to the front of the class. The two English-speaking boys were from a totally different place and didn't know the song. They told the head, but he wouldn't listen. They had worked very hard for me and always been extremely polite and co-operative. They had got on further with theory than any children in the school. I tried to explain to the head, but he was not interested. They had defied him, he thought, and he said, 'I shall write on your reports that you are obstinate and unco-operative in music.' It was typical of him. The boys were upset. I'd never had a moment's trouble with either of them.

The same head received an O.B.E. for outstanding service in education a year or so later. He was loathed by his staff and pupils alike – a most unpleasant man.

I left at the end of two terms and the children cried – even the naughtiest of them. I couldn't believe it. 'Don't go. We love singing. We'll be good Mrs Ta-té,' they said, but I couldn't face another winter of the nerve-wracking journey and the gruelling conditions.

The deputy head told my son some time later that they'd had three people in a fortnight to do my old job. The first one looked at the school but never came to teach. The second came twice and said she couldn't take it, the third was a man and would have stayed, but they discovered at the office that he wasn't qualified, so they terminated his job as soon as he'd begun.

I gather my two terms was an all-out record, yet I felt guilty every time I remembered their tears when I left.

It was my experience at this school which made me refuse Mr Hind's request to teach the older girls at the secondary modern. I felt I was just not capable of facing such a situation again.

I told a very dear neighbour who had been a professional accompanist in the schools for many years. She had been more recently my choir accompanist, but was at that time facing her terminal illness. She looked at me with her gentle compassionate eyes and said, 'Oh, do go and try. The girls in those schools need help more than anyone. You'll find there are some lovely girls amongst them. There always are. You can give it up if you can't cope. Ring Mr Hind and tell him you'll go.'

I didn't like refusing her request. She was the kindest of people and had been a treasure to us in spite of her long fight against cancer.

I rang up Mr Hind and asked him what the job entailed. He said he was most concerned about a group of older girls who were a special choir trained to sing in the big Town Hall concerts. Their teacher had collapsed and they had the songs and no one to coach them. I told him I didn't think I was much good with older children. 'But you did absolute marvels at the other senior school,' he said. 'You even got those big immigrant boys singing.' I said I'd go along one morning each week and try.

The following Tuesday I turned up.

The school had the reputation of needing police help every few days, girls attacking the staff with chairs, and outrageous behaviour at inter-school sports. I shook in my shoes as I entered the school. The building was in many ways a fine one, better than scores of fee-paying schools. The headmistress was a very pleasant, capable woman and the secretary a charming, helpful person from my own old school.

The noise and behaviour generally were appalling. The staff were in two groups – the older, loyal, experienced women, for whom I can find no suitable words of praise, and the birds of passage. The latter were often young and attractive and fought a mainly losing battle against extreme odds. I must hasten to say that by and large it was not quite as bad as its shocking reputation, but every week when I drove away I wondered why I kept going.

My first session was quite pleasant. I was shown into the music room and the special choir was sent for. They were girls of thirteen and fourteen, very mature physically. Some of them had beautiful voices, one in particular. I had just got under weigh with the festival songs – quite thrilling part-songs – when Mr Hind turned up. He was delighted that I had kept my word and we worked together with the girls for a time. He then asked if I'd like a pianist. The accompaniments were quite difficult to sight read and I thought an extra adult might be of help if I had behaviour problems, so I said it would be welcome. He proved a very mixed blessing.

To start with, his sight was poor, and his sight-reading worse than mine. He immediately began larking about with the girls, and made them excited and very cheeky. On the occasions when he didn't turn up I had a much more peaceful time. On one occasion I marched off an exceedingly insolent and destructive girl to the headmistress. When I returned the other girls were clamouring round him trying to sit on his knees.

It was not the special choir that I usually had trouble with, but the big classes of twelve and thirteen-year-olds whom I taught the rest of the morning. They were blue murder. Many of them had very tragic backgrounds. My star singer in the special choir was one of a big family. Her mother was dead, and her older sisters out working. She ran the house and looked after the younger children. In fact her younger sister was in the school and came to my lessons much cleaner and better cared-for than the average girl in the school. After a school concert I was introduced to the father and a little under-school-age brother. The father looked an inadequate type, but was obviously proud of his daughter's lovely voice. He had an Irish accent and the weakness for alcohol which often goes with it. To the delight of his daughters he met up with a woman who agreed to marry him and mother his family. The girls were very fond of her and the eldest ones went off with the happy couple to celebrate the engagement. There was a car crash and the bride-to-be was killed outright. My singer went completely hysterical, and all the older girls refused to talk to their dad because he'd killed their new mother before she'd come to them. It was a most tragic affair. Because of her home responsibilities she was very unreliable. The pianist offered to give her piano lessons in the hope that she might have a real opportunity of developing her gift, but she had always an excuse for not co-operating. The headmistress was very kind to her and towards others from difficult homes, but in many cases their anti-social behaviour made teaching them well-nigh impossible. I had been told repeatedly that if I had any trouble I must send the girls to the head's room, but as often as not if I did this the culprit would be back a bit later with a paper to sign or collecting subscriptions for something. It was obvious that no punishment had been meted out, and the girl was one up on those whose behaviour had been slightly less odious.

I trained a junior choir with great success and we had a marvellous criticism at the inter-schools' music festival. They were as keen as mustard and we had very good sessions usually. The sad thing was that as these same girls became a year older they changed beyond recognition, and the two who had worked most keenly for me would pass me in the corridor without a sign of recognition. It is a terrible sensation to be met with a stony stare from someone who has hung on your every word a few months earlier.

The third time I trained the special choir for the big Carol Concert at the Town Hall the music came through from the office in penny numbers and then often only one copy. I waited in vain for copies of the words to be typed and duplicated by the over-worked secretary. The pianist and I were trying to work from one copy and he was very rocky on the question of time. Extremely difficult three-part songs were chosen, and my pupils were not really capable of holding the lines, but I slogged away. To crown all, the teachers of the oldest and most capable singers often kept them away from their choir rehearsals to work for exams. I finally received the copies of words for the girls on the morning when several other school choirs were coming to rehearse with us. I found that all the other teachers were as beset and bothered as I was owing to shortage of copies and so on. When the girls finally turned up at the Town Hall they were all lumped together, in spite of their protests that they'd learned three different parts. They were very disgruntled about it.

That was too much for me. I blew my top and refused to coach them again. I had worked extremely hard and prepared a special item for the school concert in the summer. In spite of the staff's swearing me down that the girls were incapable of memorizing parts and singing without copies we had finally produced a very creditable performance of the 'Emperor and the Nightingale'. The art mistress had done wonders for the set, and her husband had managed to borrow beautiful costumes for us from the training college. The girls were beside themselves with delight, and waited in the TV room – blacked-out against the stares of the local louts – in elaborate costumes on the hottest evening I ever remember. The sad thing was that after the endless wait to go on stage the 'nightingale' had stage-fright. She was a tubby girl with a very good voice. She was to sing from behind the beautifully-contrived bush, but I heard a sniffle and a sob at the end of the opening chorus. The girls all looked at me in anguish, and I took up the lead and imitated the voice of the 'nightingale'. I sang the first verse and then she joined in and took over and we finished in fine style with tremendous applause. Only the pianist and the head mistress knew what had happened, apart from the girls themselves. They had done their utmost after the early mishap.

The English mistress was backstage, and when I said to her afterwards, 'It was a near thing,' she didn't know what I was talking about, and swore me down the girl had sung every note.

I asked the child why she was so nervous, and she said it was her Mam she was afraid of. Her Mam sang in 'clubs and things' and she'd been sitting in the front row. When the 'nightingale' peeped through her bush at the audience the sight of her mother had frightened her.

The last I saw of the girl she had changed very much for the worse. She had wanted to stay on at school and take a special course, but her mother and step-father had insisted that she must leave as soon as possible and start earning. She lost all interest in singing and everything else, and came to school unwashed and unkempt. She would co-operate with no one. What a pity!

In my last term I dressed my best singers in Victorian costumes and put on a 'soirée' of nostalgic songs. It was great fun, and they looked very splendid. When they asked what they'd do next year I felt very mean, but

I'd done about three years and I was worn out. My sessions with the difficult big classes were getting more and more traumatic. My old angina was reminding me of its presence, and I knew that losing my temper with the girls was dangerous. The pianist assured me that the other teacher who did a bit of singing had a much rougher house than I had, but I felt I was becoming like the girls I most deplored. I had done as much as I could for as long as I could, and the new headmaster at Bishop Bank wanted me to take Music Making as well as Singing. He arranged for me to do the extra morning there the following year. I made my farewells, and many of the staff expressed their envy. By that time my dear friend who had persuaded me to go was dead, but I think she would have agreed that I'd done my bit. She was right – some of the girls I met there were amongst the most pleasant I've ever taught, but I was very sorry for them when they had to live through their school days in the company of others who were so objectionable and who did their utmost to ruin every lesson.

I once asked the naughtiest ones to write an essay for me on why they behaved so badly in school. They said they wouldn't if all the teachers were strict, and they knew it was stupid because they wouldn't get good jobs if they did badly in their exams. Even the naughtiest enjoyed our occasional hymn sessions. It was sad that the head was not a Christian. I'm sure that the whole school would have benefited from such an influence at the top. A young woman who came to take over R.E. was shattered by her experiences at first, but she battled on and did a great deal of good amongst the girls. When I got the whole school really singing carols there was an electric atmosphere and the staff expressed surprise that the girls were capable of singing like that. I had to coax and tease them to break down their defences and then the result was very exciting.

It would seem strange to one who had never taught that I could have found one half day a week such an enormous strain. I always dreaded going, worked absolutely flat out and left the building feeling completely exhausted, but I doubt whether anyone excepting the pianist knew how much it cost me. As at the other senior school the children were upset when they knew I was leaving, and the headmistress particularly so. She was kind enough to say that she had always looked to me to put a shine on their concerts, and that it was incredible that I achieved so much in my few hours there.

The new head at Bishop Bank kept assuring me that he was going to speak to Mr Hind and arrange the prospective change. When I heard later on that Mr Hind was completely ignorant of the situation I was puzzled and realized only two years later that there were two Mr Hinds. The second one was in charge of the First Schools and as Bishop Bank was to change to one, he was the man consulted. So, most unfortunately, it appeared that I had lied to the headmistress and been very discourteous to the Mr Hind I knew. Every time I suggested that I ought to contact him I was told not to do so, as it was the responsibility of the headmaster of Bishop Bank. I'm always hoping I'll bump into the secretary or headmistress and clear my name on that score.

Whilst I was battling away with the older girls I was still spending three half days at Bishop Bank. There were always children watching for my arrival, opening the car and school door and wanting to help. When I put my nose into the staffroom there were four pairs of eyes with a special gleam in them and, 'Me today. Glad to see you,' on their lips. How they prized their half hour break when I took their classes! I was very fond of them all. They were a wonderfully happy team, and very appreciative of each other's support and co-operation. Mr Stroller's influence permeated the place, of course, but the deputy head was an extremely friendly and capable man – loved by the staff and children alike. He would have made a very good headmaster, but he liked teaching too much to give it up in favour of administration. The senior mistress was an outstandingly good teacher. Although she had trained for infants she loved the challenge of teaching juniors and never tired of giving every ounce of herself to her job. I always saw an amazing improvement in the children who went into her class. Their general responsiveness and manners reflected her influence, and they were a joy to handle. She taught them Scottish dancing in the dinner hour and we sometimes took a team to dance and sing at one of the old people's homes. The children loved to go, and would buy sweets for the old people and go and chat to them in the most natural way when their entertainment was over.

Young teachers fresh from College always appreciated the help and encouragement given by the senior members of the staff. We had cards or notes of appreciation at the end of the probationary year. One young teacher – now headmaster of a lovely country school – told me he learnt more in a term at Bishop Bank than in three years at College. He followed the deputy head round with a notebook as often as possible, and asked his advice when his ears and eyes couldn't supply all the answers. At their joint class party the two of them disappeared and came back later dressed as Spanish dancers – the young one dressed as a woman with a black wig. They did a very stylish tango to the roars of delight from the children. They managed to get all the boys as well as the girls doing old-tyme dances. There were always fancy-dress competitions and hat-making competitions on these feast days, and the imagination and originality displayed were marvellous. The standard of handwork was extremely high, fostered by the deputy head's ordering of masses of beautiful craft material and his constant good example. On open days the school was a showpiece.

CHAPTER FIFTEEN

THE END IN SIGHT

The death knell of the wonderfully happy team began with Mr Stroller's retirement and the announcement that the school would have to change to a First School over the next two years. The deputy head stayed on an extra year in order to see the new headmaster settled in, and throughout his last year the old staff were gradually seeking other posts for when the age groups changed. They were very unhappy. It was the end of an era for us all. It meant specializing and teaching older children for them. Most of them were very much happier in the existing set-up, teaching most subjects but giving extra help to others when necessary. It is a much more interesting life. I was the only one teaching one subject only, but having ten classes to teach I had plenty of variety.

However, my voice took a great deal of punishment. I was often very croaky by the end of a session, and H. was afraid I'd lose my voice altogether. I knew from experience that it usually came back, unless I'd picked up a germ in addition to the ordinary strain. I became more and more depressed as the end of the year approached. The previous summer I had been asked by the deputy head and the senior mistress not to let the choir sing 'Will ye no' come back again?' when Mr Stroller came to give the prizes. They had come to me individually with the same request and each had added, 'You'll have the whole school in tears.' I wondered how I was going to say 'Goodbye' to all my colleagues without breaking down. But their last day was brilliantly sunny and the fancy dress parade was out of doors, followed by staff-versus-children rounders and dancing to gramophone records. I went the rounds and shook their hands, wishing them all well in their new schools. We all swore to meet again for a meal in the autumn, and not to let our friendships slide. We've met several times and it is like a big family

Author with Hal and son Chris, 1991.

reunion.

Two women teachers who shared a class stayed on. They knew that part-time jobs were almost impossible to get. In contrast to when I had gone back to teaching there were now young trained teachers without jobs. I had agreed to stay on, as I loved young children and had trained to handle them.

In the autumn I went back to Bishop Bank through a group of mothers and tiny children. It was like turning back the clock, but only to a very limited degree. Most of the new staff were trained for juniors and when they were eventually obliged to teach infants it was like learning a new language. As the old staff had done, they brought their children to me to teach in the hall. Under Mr Stroller the catering staff had been obliged to be out of their end of the hall before I began teaching. Illness and general disgruntlement had led to a lowering of morale and efficiency. My two afternoon sessions began with the ladies still chattering and banging at the far end of the hall and then their echoing voices as they had their own meal there. The young children had now all been handled on the 'do-as-you-darned-well-please' principle and were naturally inclined to chatter, fidget and play. Controlling them and teaching them in a room constantly echoing with other sounds was almost impossible.

'New' ideas were being adopted by people at the top, who, in their complete ignorance imagined that singing could be taught at one end of the room whilst C stream children were taught to bake at the other. A mother of four children had been bringing her little four-year-old daughter with her and helping with the lower juniors' needlework two afternoons each week. She now found herself trying to handle difficult children at the dining end of the hall with me teaching singing in the same room. I was bitterly sorry for her. The children waiting their turn to make their cakes went wild, and she was harassed to death. It took her a good half hour to clear up when the rest of the staff had departed, and the two of us were like rags by the end of the afternoon. After a term of it I went on strike and said I couldn't teach with all the shindy going on, but in the meantime the head had brought in a contingent of starry-eyed teachers to see how open-planning worked in Bishop Bank!

I was used to visitors. Overseas visitors came very often in the old days and I was always glad to welcome them to my classes, but I didn't want anyone to think I was a party to the lunatic ideas being introduced into teaching to the chagrin of ninety-nine per cent of the experienced teachers. I knew of too many teachers retiring early and whole staffs leaving schools because of the ridiculous ideas being forced on them.

I began to teach some of my music making in the classrooms until the noise in the hall had subsided. I saw then why my little charges were so completely wild. Many of them sat facing the wall or a cupboard placed between them and the teacher's desk. It took me ages to get them sitting so that I could see them all, and they could look at me without twisting round in their seats. The teacher of one class – a history graduate – told me she'd never seen her children all doing anything together until I took them! She was building her teaching skills on what was being practised by the new senior assistant, whose children were the wildest in the school. I was aghast at what I saw, and decided that I would gear my teaching to getting them to listen and respond. It was something they'd never done.

All children love music making, and the lessons were never long enough. By the time I'd trundled all my gear into the room, sorted out the children and given out the instruments I knew that another lot of children would be waiting for me. In the hall I taught them to listen to the piano and do what it told them to do – walking, running, skipping, swinging, going to sleep and so on. I made up stories full of actions about different creatures in a variety of situations. With the older ones we used instruments of different pitch, and made sound patterns representing people in the stories. They began to recognise notes in the sol-fa scale and to sing intervals to hand signs. We learned numbers of nursery rhymes and did dances and actions to them. They loved it all and never wanted to go.

My biggest problem was that under the new regime the ages of the bottom three classes were scrambled, so that I had no hope of building a proper scheme of work. A four-year-old little girl is quite a different creature from a six-to-seven-year-old boy. It was natural that the latter would be restless and scornful if work was geared to the former. It was equally natural that the tiny ones were lost and at sea with what suited the older ones.

The idiots who thought up vertical streaming had never tried to apply it to music. When asked by a close friend of mine if it could be done, the music lecturer at a well-known College said it was impossible.

I'm not idle, nor unimaginative, but I'm not fool enough to carry on doing the impossible.

The two ladies who shared a class – extremely capable efficient teachers – were by this time going dotty over the slipping standards in the school. They told me they were leaving. Until then I had not seriously considered resigning.

Most of the new staff I liked and got on well with, but the senior assistant was a second Mrs Potts and had put everyone's back up. Her complete lack of sympathy over the real needs of the little ones made me see red. She was constantly thinking of ambitious schemes and then leaving all the donkey work for others to do. As often as not her children were left in the hands of the young nursery assistant. I had agreed to taking all the youngest children for a hymn practice at the end of Thursday afternoon as long as one teacher came to watch the children when I was playing. They ended by being a nightmare, especially in bad weather when the children had been kept indoors all day. They came in like animals let out into the fields for the first time in spring. Having seen them in – sometimes as many as a hundred and thirty altogether – the teachers faded out and the poor nursery assistant was left. She could not control them and the naughtiest were never really under control anyway. I found my head getting more and more painful. I hate having to shout at children, but speaking was useless. The sessions became an endurance test.

I decided to make my bow.

The head was desolate, and said he had an American professor coming over especially to see my wonderful work. I made as many excuses as I could – all of them true – and in the end said that I thought the so-called 'modern' ideas were a reversion to dame-school teaching, and a breeding ground for hooligans.

I thought of the happy years with the old staff and the lively and responsive juniors, of the children I'd taught to read music and play recorders, glockenspiels and so on, of the mad noisy 'band' sessions with

Robert Studley – who gave the title to this book.

the C children, which had nearly split my head but satisfied them immensely, and of the tiny ones dancing round the little nut tree. It was a big wrench to end it all, but my old heart kept reminding me of its presence, and I knew in my bones I ought to finish teaching.

They gave me dozens of beautiful roses in a reproduction Georgian silver rose bowl. I gave them a lovely tree I'd grown from seed and said I'd go back to help in an emergency.

Now I'm at home. Eric, Doug and Alf have all died in the last eleven months. My old angina has been more of a nuisance than ever since it reared its ugly head thirty-six years ago. Perhaps I'll have more energy later on. If not I must be thankful for all the fun I've had over the years.

I've still my choir and we sing regularly to cheer up those even older and more infirm, and I've still the little ones in the Primary at Sunday School to remind me that I'm NOBBUT A LIDLE SKEEAL TAICHER.